FROM WILLING SUB TO ENSLAVED CAPTIVE

BY

SCARLETT FLAME

SCARLETT FLAME

LEGAL NOTES

CHAPTER 1

It was only two weeks until Christmas and I was at a party, at the BDSM club *Substation*, with my new Dom, Charles. But I was feeling down.

We had been seeing each other for a couple of months, now, and I was uneasy about our relationship. Initially, it had worked well, as he appeared to be very considerate, and we sort of gelled after playing at a local munch.

I was "under consideration", as it is worded in the world of BDSM and the Lifestyle. This meant that we weren't committed to each other, yet, and I wasn't technically collared. I did wear a collar when we played, or visited a club or munch, but there was no padlock, or key to it.

It was a play collar and others might have worn it before me. I wasn't sure.

Yet, whilst I was "under consideration", a verbal agreement had been negotiated, so that neither of us would play with, or have sex with any others, and limits were assured.

I had been looking for a Dom/sub relationship for some years, and I was no spring chicken. Maybe this would be my last chance to find my *one*.

Charles' looks belied his nature, as he was baby-faced; some would say, almost pretty, with dark brown hair, chocolate brown eyes, and clean shaven. Dimples appeared when he smiled. No blemishes, or pock marks marred his smooth complexion, and he sported a natural-looking golden tan, all year around.

In contrast, his true character was dark and troubled. Charles was tall, approximately six feet two inches, lean, and with a naturally-toned look.

What had happened to make him so sadistic and unfeeling at times? Why were his aggressive tendencies so extreme? Something must have happened in the past to make him derive so much pleasure from inflicting pain and humiliation.

Although I am a masochist, and spanking and flogging get my juices flowing, I wouldn't describe myself as a pain-slut by any means.

We were now friends on Fetworld, and I had changed my status to reflect the fact that I was under consideration.

This was a red flag to all the other Doms, switches and kinksters, letting them know that I was considering entering a more committed relationship with Charles.

We had been out for the odd meal initially, but that was more a way to get together to discuss the parameters of our current relationship.

Unlike in 50 Shades, many of these negotiations are verbal. I had only ever had the mention of a written contract on two previous occasions.

I knew of a few wealthy Doms, but very few could be described as playboy billionaires! The vast majority of the Dominant men and women I knew were more likely to be in either the police force, (I kid you not!), the NHS – Yes doctors and nurses are very likely to play kinky doctors and nurses in real life, accountants, and all manner of professions. It is true to say that the dominant ones are generally at the top of the chain of command, though, although the opposite is also true.

Oh, I forgot to mention the armed forces, which also provide any number of Doms and subs in the Lifestyle.

But, I digress.

It is also nonsense that these clubs and munches don't serve alcohol in the UK. But, if you had any sense, you would avoid getting plastered as your pain receptors and your perception of pain would be skewed.

My Dom was sat in a nice comfy chair, and I, as usual, knelt alongside. I was wearing the black play collar, short, black leather skirt, and an under bust corset. My nipples had clamps with little silver bells on, attached to the tender little peaks. I wore no panties. This is par for the course, as Doms generally like their submissive's to be available to them at all times.

My head was bowed, and I was mulling over the events of the weeks since we had met, and agreed to see if we were compatible.

Charles seemed very happy with the arrangement so far, and I could tell he was already anticipating collaring me, but I knew that the chances of that happening were slim and that I was more than likely to refuse his collar.

His previous partners had not been submissive's, but slaves.

A slave is a very different kettle of fish to the role of submissive, I might add. I had no intention of becoming anybody's slave.

I was being treated more and more like a possession, with each subsequent play session. My limits were being pushed hard with each one.

I glanced up, and noticed a dour-faced man, standing near the bar. He was handsome, but in an understated way.

I knew I shouldn't, but I couldn't help checking him out.

He had dark hair, very neat except for a cowlick that seemed untameable. I couldn't help but think of Superman.

He looked up and our eyes connected. It was akin to a lightning bolt hitting my body and I caught my breath. My pussy clenched in response.

He had piercing blue eyes, and his right cheek was marred by a thick keloid scar running through it. Instead of making him less attractive, it seemed to throw the rest of his features into sharper contrast. Dark-haired, clean-shaven, with a chiselled chin. He was wearing Dom black. Seems to be a bit of a trend with Doms. Black leather figure-hugging pants, black shirt with what appeared to be black boots. Over this he wore a black leather sleeveless vest.

Some Doms wore this outfit better than others. He wore the look well.

I dipped my gaze, as I was a little unnerved that he continued to stare so blatantly, and I was pretty certain he spotted my reaction.

I went back to considering my future, contemplating my current situation once more. I needed to end this relationship with Charles, and soon.

It was at that moment I realised that Charles had been talking to me, and I had been blanking him out. In my defence, this was partly because the club was so bloody noisy. Everyone was getting excited as Christmas drew near. Everyone, except me!

I looked to Charles and he reached out and grabbed a fistful of my long dark hair and yanked my head back sharply, jarring my neck in the process.

Now, generally, having my hair grabbed is on my fetish list, and one of my *things*. But this was so violent the effect was akin to whiplash.

I gasped, not in pleasure but in acute pain, and made to grab at his hand to ease it back when my hand was slapped away, furiously.

This was followed swiftly by a loud slap to my face. If his hand hadn't still been in my hair, I would have fallen to the floor. Now slapping isn't good, in my book, but it startled me and I dropped my hand away to clutch at my now-flaming cheeks.

"Sweetheart," he snarled, "I was talking to you. In fact, I asked the same question three times."

I lowered my eyes a little, unable to look directly into his narrowed gaze.

"Yes, Sir. Sorry, Sir. "I said. It wasn't worth retaliating but, at the same time, I knew that my status would be changing to single upon my return home. And a certain Dom would be blocked, and un-friended.

"I asked, are you ready to play, my sweet? As I see the spanking bench is free? "

My eyes gravitated, of their own accord, to the area behind him, which was designated the dungeon. Sure enough, the bench was clear.

He grabbed my upper arm, digging his fingers in hard, and yanked me to my feet.

That was going to leave a few bruises, I thought.

At this point, I was getting more than a little worried, as I could see that he was enraged.

Anger is not an emotion to use in play, and I was becoming alarmed, and terrified of the consequences of my inattention.

He dragged me along to the bench and I couldn't help but resist. I just knew this would end in tears, and not the good kind.

We reached the bench, and I hoped that one of the dungeon masters would be watching: unfortunately for me, it didn't seem to be the case.

This scene had already begun to go downhill fast, and 'Red', the universal safe word, was on the tip of my tongue.

Charles obviously anticipated this, and out of his jacket pocket he produced a ball gag which he swiftly forced into my mouth.

I could feel myself tearing up, and the waterworks weren't far away. I tried to shake my head no, but Charles gripped my hair and yanked... Hard.

Tears were streaming down my face, and drool had quickly begun to pool around the gag. My nose was dripping: not a pretty sight, by any means.

My eyes widened in terror.

What the actual fuck? I thought.

Just as I was thinking *I am well and truly stuffed, and this is going to end badly*, Charles appeared to fly backwards through the air, in slow motion.

At that point, both dungeon masters appeared, as if by magic. They restrained Charles physically as I stood there, stunned. They began to escort him off towards the main entrance, Charles struggling and shouting curses the whole time. At that instant, I could sense someone behind me, who then proceeded to undo the straps on the gag.

Time caught up with me and, as the gag was removed, I began to turn to see who was coming to my aid.

As I turned, I began to sway and the room began to pitch. I faltered. Flight or fight had caught up with me, and my eyes began to roll back in my head as darkness descended.

CHAPTER 2

I awoke, unsure how long I had been out of it, I was in what I went on to discover was the office at the club, on someone's lap, with a soft blanket draped over me.

I looked up and recognised my saviour straightaway. Those vivid blue eyes were unmistakeable.

"Shh… Take your time, and have a few sips of water."

A bottle was gently placed against my lips, and he held his hands around mine to steady them as he tipped it up.

I sipped, gratefully as my throat was so dry and parched.

He waited until I had finished drinking, then carefully wiped my mouth with a cotton handkerchief. He dabbed at my lips, gingerly.

"Thank you. Thank you so much." I whimpered. As I spoke, I felt some pain in the corners of my mouth, and tentatively touched them. Charles must have split the skin when he drove the gag into place so forcibly. Fresh tears began to fall.

"Let it all out, Little One." My white knight softly told me. "I have you. No one will hurt you again tonight, and your Dom has been informed that he is no longer welcome here."

I caught my breath and began to slowly relax. I was safe for now, and with luck would never hear from Charles again.

Although I had been to Charles's home twice, he didn't have my home address.

Once my breathing had evened out, and my tears subsided, my saviour allowed me to sit up. I climbed off his knee and moved to the chair opposite, as he regarded me intently. I pulled the blanket tighter around me.

"That bastard has hurt your mouth. It should heal quite quickly, though. I'm not sure what you had done that deserved that kind of behaviour, but any true Dom never punishes his sub in anger. If punishment is deserved, it should be delivered when tempers are under control," he said. "Now, how are you feeling? And, most importantly, how are you going to get home?"

"Well, I can get a taxi home from here, and I am feeling much better now, thank you. The first thing I will do is notify my ex-Dom of my new status. Single. Then I will be blocking him. I think it is the best thing to do in the circumstances."

"I will order you a taxi, or, if you think you can trust me, I can drop you off at your home. Do you live far?

"I live about twenty minutes away from here but, please, don't put yourself out. I am sure that I can make my own way home. You have done so much for me already. I hate to think what Charles would have done if he had managed to secure me to that bench."

"In that case, I will order you a taxi but if I could ask that you become my friend on Fetworld. That way I can be sure that you get home safe and sound. You can message me to let me know that you have arrived home."

"Thank you. I am happy to do that. My name is SuzieQ on Fetworld." I responded. I got my mobile out as he began to scroll through his phone.

I then saw a friend request pop up from a Dr_Strict.

I raised my eyebrows and enquired, "Dr_Strict?"

"Yes. That's me. I am a consultant surgeon, at one of the local hospitals."

"Interesting," I replied. "I am a student nurse, locally, too."

"Really?"

"Yes. St Winifred's, down the road. Do you know it? Well, that is my current placement, in any case."

"I know of it, but I am based elsewhere. We may bump into one another when you rotate for your placements, though."

We both stood, and I asked, "Can I know your name, Sir? Mine is Suzie, as you may have guessed"

"No. No, not at all. It is Simon Traynor. Nice to meet you, Suzie." And he proceeded to shake my hand.

Simon escorted me to the cloakroom to retrieve my coat and went so far as to fasten the buttons for me. We exited the building together and my taxi was waiting outside, having arrived promptly.

Simon had a few words with the driver, then we parted company after a few hastily said goodbyes.

As I sat in the taxi on the way home I ran through the events of the evening, over and over in my head trying to make sense of it all, to no avail.

Maybe it was time to give up my search, and settle for a vanilla relationship.

We arrived at my home, and I went to pay the driver, but he said. "No problem, Miss. Your boyfriend paid before we left."

I smiled to myself as I wondered what Simon had said to him.

"Thank you. Goodnight."

"He also said that I had to wait until you were safe inside, and to remind you to message him, and lock your front door," he said.

My smile grew, as I walked up the pathway, stepping carefully as it was frosted over and slippery.

I let myself in my front door, put the safety chain across, and bolted it from inside. A couple of minutes later, I heard the taxi pull away.

I stripped off in my bedroom and turned on the shower. After tonight's scene, I felt the need to scrub myself clean.

As I waited for the shower to heat up, I picked up my phone and sent a message to Simon, letting him know that I had got home safely, and thanking him once more for intervening on my behalf.

I then spent a good ten minutes showering, scrubbing myself almost raw in the process. I needed to scrub away Charles's touch, and remove the scent of him from my skin.

Using a towel as a turban I dried off quickly, put on my comfy dressing gown, and headed to the bedroom. I flicked the telly on, as I knew sleep would be impossible for me right now. My brain was still working overtime.

I heard a buzz from my phone to let me know that I had received a text. So, I picked it up, and sat on the bed.

It was a message from Charles.

That bastard had the nerve to text me, I thought.

I read it quickly.

Don't think you have got away without your punishment. You will meet me tomorrow evening at seven o'clock at the station. Sir.

I got up off the bed and paced around the bedroom.

I felt like I wanted to smash my phone against the wall.

"What the fuck? Who the fuck does he think he is? Delusional, that's what he is!" I shouted out loud.

"Not happening. Hell will freeze over before I meet him again. Arrgh!"

I heard another notification, and looked again. Thinking it might be another text from him, but then I realised it was a message on Fetworld, from Simon.

Glad to hear that you got home safe and sound. I was worried about you, Little One. I was also wondering if you would like to meet up for coffee. I would love to discuss something with you. Are you still looking for a relationship? If so, I would be interested in discussing this with you at length. I won't rush you after your horrible experience tonight. But, I felt we had a connection, and I would like to see if we might be compatible. Let someone else know where, and who you are meeting up with. Set up safe calls, and we will take it from there.

I lay back on my pillows, and pondered my response. What a crazy night I had, had. I'd just narrowly escaped an abusive relationship with a Dom. Did I want to risk getting into a relationship so soon after that? Yet I had to admit that my gut reaction to Simon was overwhelming, and he did save me. I also knew his name, or thought I did. I walked over to my laptop, and booted up.

Thank goodness for Google. I thought.

I typed in Dr. Simon Traynor, and immediately got a number of hits. I clicked on images and, sure enough, there he was.

He was a consultant surgeon at the nearby hospital, St Jude's. His speciality was thoracic medicine, and he appeared to be a well-respected doctor and consultant, with a private practice, as well as his NHS work.

It wouldn't hurt to go out for coffee or a bite to eat I thought.

I replied that I would love to meet him for coffee, and settled on a time and place.

I didn't reply to Charles, but did as I said I would, unfriending, and blocking him. I removed him from my status, and listed myself as single again. Finally, I blocked him on my phone and removed his details.

"Good riddance to bad rubbish." I said, out loud.

I made myself a cup of hot chocolate, put away my laptop, and placed my phone on charge.

I needed to escape reality so I put on Christmas 24, to chillax, and soon fell asleep, leaving the telly on.

Sunday morning arrived and I stretched my arms out, trying to work out the kinks I seemed to have acquired from sleeping the previous night. Again, I went over the previous evening's events and vowed never to get myself into that kind of situation again. This time, I would be more careful. I put the kettle on, and grabbed a bowl of cereal.

Back in bed, sipping my tea, I decided to ring Claire. Claire was my best friend, fellow nursing student, and submissive.

I would be able to explain everything that happened without Claire judging me, but it required a face to face meeting. It would be too difficult to explain via text or through a phone call. A catch-up with Claire seemed the ideal plan.

I sent a text, asking if she fancied going out for a bite to eat, and we arranged to meet up at our local pub for a late lunch.

Soon it was time to get ready so I dressed up warm: jeans, jumper, winter coat and my comfy boots.

I arrived at the pub on foot, and spotted Claire straight away. She was stood nattering to the barman, and I could see she had already got a bottle of our usual tipple – Shiraz - and two wine glasses.

We hugged, and found a free table near the back of the pub set cosily near the log fire they always had burning at this time of year. We ordered our usual roast beef dinners, with Yorkshire pudding.

"Hey, girlfriend. What was all the hoo-ha? I noticed you are now free and single on Fetworld and have removed that rat Charles from your status. I checked up, being the nosy bugger that I am. What happened? I know you were debating where it was going with him, but this was a bit unexpected."

I went into detail, explaining all about what had happened at the club the previous night, and about the Dom that was now my white knight.

"Suzie, you need to be careful. He is still a Dominant, you know they sometimes have their own agenda and like to be in command? Make sure you aren't jumping from the frying pan into the fire."

"I am going to meet him at seven tonight, in town, at that new café, La Tosca. He is Simon Traynor. A consultant at St Jude's, here in London. I will let you know when I have arrived safely, and you know the routine from there. You will agree to be my safe call, won't you Clair? I will check in with you every fifteen minutes, until it is time to leave. He even stipulated that I organise a safe call for this evening."

"Well, at least that sounds promising, and no worries, I've got your back. Always have, always will. Now tuck in and eat, and let me in on the rest of the goss."

We sat and chatted for hours until I realised it was time to set off. For my assignation with Dr_Strict.

I called for a taxi and we said our goodbyes, with Claire reminding me to text once I had arrived at the café-bar.

I settled into the taxi for the short ride into town. Butterflies the size of elephants were taking flight in my stomach as my nerves began to mount.

I got there a couple of minutes late, as we got stuck in traffic. Paid for my taxi, took a deep breath and headed inside.

Doms hate tardiness, and I had a feeling that this particular Dominant would be no exception.

CHAPTER 3

I spotted him almost straight away, sitting at the back, to the right-hand side, in a secluded spot.

As I started to move across the floor he rose to his feet, unsmiling.

Uh-oh, this wasn't a very auspicious start, was it? I told myself.

"Suzie." He said, abruptly.

"Simon." I answered. Then he indicated that I should sit down, adjacent to him, which I did.

There was an uncomfortable silence while he weighed me up. His severe expression was making me feel off-balance, so off-balance that I began to get to my feet.

"Where do you think you are going, Little One?" he asked. His expressionless face sealed the deal for me.

Why on earth did I come out tonight? I thought.

"Sit down, now, and listen to what I have to say. If, at the end of our conversation, you don't like my proposal, you can then walk away. Just hear me out."

I stood there for a minute or two more before I finally decided: "In for a penny, in for a pound."

The least I could do was stay and hear him out. He had rescued me the previous evening, and paid for my taxi fare home, after all.

Finally, I sat down and looked over at him, cocking my head to await what he had to say.

"Okay. But, if I don't like what I hear I am off out of here."

Simon called over to the waitress and ordered drinks, then began his proposals.

"Suzie, first of all, what is it you want? Can you tell me, succinctly? What is your heart's desire in regard to the Lifestyle?"

Now, this might seem like a simple question but, as a submissive, I always found telling a Dom what I wanted was so very difficult.

I hummed and haa'd a bit, and finally thought: *Hell, yeah. Go for it. I have always balked at letting a Dom know what I really wanted, before now. I always just adapted to their wants and needs. Maybe it was now time to lay my cards on the table, and up my game.*

I still couldn't look him in the eye, though, and said.

"I really want something that covers both vanilla, and a D/s relationship. Where it is 24/7, but not so obvious to my family, but I'm still able to be submissive in subtle ways. I know it is a big ask, though."

The coffees arrived and we sat quietly, as Simon continued to study me closely. Finally, he sighed loudly, and then replied. "Then we are on the same page. I am ready to commit to the right submissive, but I will require a total TPE in the bedroom."

I looked up in astonishment.

A TPE, or Total Power Exchange, is a huge commitment, and not one I was sure that I could manage, or commit to. To give myself entirely to someone… I had no doubt that I was a submissive, but this could be a step too far.

"Suzie, would you be willing to at least try, and see where this takes us both? I realise that you have broken up from university for the Christmas holidays, and I am now on holiday for the next three weeks also. This would be an ideal time to commit, and see what happens."

"Message your friend that you are still okay, and not to worry."

I couldn't believe that I had forgotten to message Claire, and let her know that I had arrived safely.

"Yes." I nodded assent.

" Pardon?" Simon replied.

"Yes, I want to try this. I would like to see where this goes."

"Fine," Simon said. "Before we discuss this any further, have you had any contact from Charles? Despite your lack of concern, he didn't seem to come across as someone that would easily let go."

"I got a text from him last night funnily enough. He told me that I had to meet him tonight at seven at the station, and that he still intended to punish me."

"I made some enquires from fellow Doms and establishments he frequented. It seems that Charles has a bit of a reputation, and not a particularly good one. All you need to know is that I will protect you, and you are not to worry. Understand? Now let's start on the right foot. From this moment on you will call me Sir when you address me Little One. We will discuss further protocol, limits and fine details tomorrow. Do you live alone, Little One? I would like you to move in with me, if all goes to plan over the Christmas holidays."

"I do live alone, but I am not sure about moving in together so soon, Sir."

"Don't worry, Little One, the decision will be yours to make. Now then, would you like to have something to eat, and stop and chat, or have you other plans for tonight?"

"I would love to spend some time here, getting to know each other, Sir."

Simon called the waitress over, requesting menus and with food ordered, we continued chatting.

The conversation, for the most part, was about me: where I was from, my ambitions, my family and hobbies.

By the end of the meal I had relaxed so much I had forgotten to call Simon "Sir" on several occasions. He said nothing, but I could see by his facial expressions that the omissions had been noted. I debated internally what punishment I would receive for these misdemeanours, clenching my thighs, partly in trepidation, and partly in anticipation. Only time would tell.

"Well, Little Miss. Time you returned home to bed. A good night's sleep for you, my dear. You haven't stopped yawning for the last ten minutes or so, and it is contagious. You had a traumatic time last night, and I imagine sleep was a little elusive."

"Yes, Sir." I yawned as I replied. "I hadn't realised how much it had taken out of me. That, and the red wine I had this afternoon, and again tonight, have knocked me for six, Sir."

Simon rose, and walked around the table. He had already insisted on paying the bill, muttering something about student bursaries to himself.

He took my coat from the waitress, and held it out for me. Once again, he insisted on fastening it up. I felt very spoiled. I generally didn't do Daddy Doms and littles, but I kind of liked all this attention.

Such a contrast to Charles. I just had to hope that like Charles, this caring attention didn't dry up as we continued to see each other.

I got a ping again on my phone and realised that I had been so absorbed in our conversation, that I hadn't let Claire know that I was all right.

Simon, smiled, then said, "I am glad your friend is so diligent. Let her know that you are still in one piece, and about to head home, Little One."

I duly sent Claire a text

Heading home now. Had a great evening, just chatting. No playing, and been in the public eye all night.

"Good girl." Simon said and I stood a little taller. How come those two little words mean so much to me and all my submissive friends?

He placed his right hand on the small of my back, and guided me to the front door asking,

"Now then, Little Miss, will it be a taxi again tonight? Or will you allow me the satisfaction of driving you home and being sure you arrive there, safe and sound?"

I was still not quite sure to be perfectly honest. My recent experiences with Charles had eaten away at my trust. Yet I had agreed to embark on a relationship of sorts with Simon. So, I replied, honestly. "I would like you to take me home, Sir. Although I am still wary. After my recent troubles, this is a hard decision but I feel that I can trust you, and must tell you that I Googled your name last night. To check that what you told me was the truth. To confirm you were who you said you were, Sir."

"Clever Girl. Always be truthful and honest with me, and I will reciprocate in kind. Trust, honesty, and consensual, safe and sane play."

We walked out of the restaurant and across to the car park. I saw lights flash and was led to a jaguar XF, in cherry red. Gleaming under the street lights.

"OMG! How cool is this?" I squealed.

Simon let me go, and stepped forward to open the passenger door. I climbed inside.

He entered the driver's side and leaned over across to make sure my seatbelt was securely fastened His proximity was causing my heart to race, and my palms turned sweaty. I inhaled his unique fragrance. A combination of musk, and the undertones of his expensive aftershave, accompanied by the warmth of his body, so close to mine, overwhelmed me.

I gasped, and my core clenched in response. My juices were now flowing freely.

Simon turned to me once more and inhaled, tipping his head back slightly and to one side as if scenting the air.

I smiled, nervously, as Simon's face lit up with a beatific smile.

"Hmmm. What a lovely aroma, my Little One. I can't wait to taste you. I hope you taste as sweet as that tantalising scent."

I felt myself redden and dropped my gaze, realising the blush extended down to my chest.

"Nothing to be embarrassed about, my Sweet. This signifies that the attraction that I felt for you is mutual. Your aromatic response tells me so much. I couldn't have asked for a better response. I would happily fuck you across the bonnet of this car as a Dominant. But, as a gentleman, I will wait until we know each other better, and I have earned your trust."

He started the car and asked, "Where is home, Little One? Are you able to direct me, or have you a postcode for my satnav?"

I took a deep breath, exhaled nervously, and said "Turn left out of the car park, Sir. I will direct you."

He carefully negotiated the turn, and sped off. Before too long we were pulling up in front of my little two-up two-down terraced house. Nothing special, but I called it home.

Before I could even react, and reach for the door, I wondered what Simon would think of my little house, he had rushed around, and was opening my door.

He held my hand as he assisted me out of the car, and walked me up to my door.

He continued to hold my hand as we stood there, then let go and moved a step back.

"I will message you my mobile number, and you will then text me yours. Sleep tight, my Little One, and tomorrow we will meet once more and spend time together. Get to know each other. We have a lot to discuss, and negotiations to make. Make a list of your soft limits, a separate list of your existing fetishes, and those you are curious to try. Sleep tight, and sweet dreams."

"Good night, Sir. I will make the lists tomorrow, and look forward to seeing you again. Thank you for a lovely evening, Sir."

He picked up my hand and turned it over, placing a gentle kiss on the palm. Goosebumps broke out all over the surface of my skin, and the hair on the back of my neck stood on end.

Simon waited until I had my keys in my hand, held his hand out palm up and I handed him the correct key, then stepped aside as he opened the door and held it for me.

I flicked on the lights in my hallway and stepped inside, as he handed me back the keys.

"I will wait until I hear you lock and bolt the door, then head off. Once again, sweet dreams and I will see you tomorrow."

I closed the door, locked, bolted and put the safety chain on, then I leant back against the door and closed my eyes. I could hear his footsteps retreating up the path. Two minutes later I heard him pull away.

Wow! I thought to myself. *I can't wait for tomorrow to arrive.*

My head was buzzing and I went into the kitchen to make a drink of warm milk. I doubted if I would sleep, again, after today's events. I thought I would probably go over and over it all in my mind.

But I was wrong. I drank my milk after undressing, settled into my bed, and quickly dropped off into a deep sleep.

CHAPTER 4

With no Uni, or placement until after Christmas, I hadn't set an alarm but awoke to my phone ringing. I could tell from the ringtone that is was Claire. I grabbed the phone off the bedside table and spent the next half hour discussing how well my *date* had gone.

Claire was cock-a-hoop, but also reminded me to take care and reminded me that if I did decide to take him up on his offer, I should not forget her over Christmas. I agreed to let her know exactly where he lived, in case of emergencies.

I took a pen and notepad out of my bag and set it on the coffee table in the living room.

Then I put on some toast and made a cup of tea. I intended to commence my first task for Simon over breakfast.

I took a swig of tea and a big bite of my buttered toast, and pondered over what to write.

I began with my hard limits, as they were easy to list. Then my soft limits. Those could be pushed by my Dom. I was shocked at the size of my list of fetishes. Spanking, flogging, bondage, and particularly rope, such as Shibari, right at the top.

The hardest part of my lists to compile was the one where I had to admit to myself the fetishes I was curious about. Happy with my completed lists, I set them aside and looked at my messages, sure enough, Simon had sent me his mobile number.

I entered it on to my phone and saved it. Then, I texted

Good morning, Sir.

I put the kettle on, and it hadn't even begun to boil when I heard the ping of a message. A smile spread across my face, as it was Simon wishing me good morning and asking was I available to talk on the phone. I responded straight away.

Yes, Sir.

I was just about to pour the boiling water into my mug when I jumped on hearing the phone ring.

I answered with "Hello, Sir." And we began to talk in earnest.

Simon wanted to meet for lunch at another local restaurant that day in order to talk further. At this rate, I would be the size of a house come Christmas Day, eating out so many times, but I readily agreed.

Before he rang off, Simon gave me another task. I wasn't too shocked at getting given a task, as this was par for the course for a submissive: a way to test, and to keep on testing the connection, and the sub's willingness to submit. He asked me not to wear panties this evening, and requested that I wear a skirt, stockings and suspenders. To be quite honest, this is a very common request, and I had no shortage of stockings and suspenders to choose from.

I looked through my wardrobe and quickly gathered a garter, and a pair of lace topped stockings with a matching lacy bra. I spent quite a while deciding on which skirt to wear and opted for a black pencil skirt, with a walking slit up the back, and a silky, button-though blue-striped blouse.

The hardest part came when I tried to finish dressing. I was shaking so much in nervous anticipation that I found it almost impossible to fasten my stockings. In fact, I had to refasten them several times before I got it right.

Simon had told me to be ready and waiting at half past twelve. He was due to message me upon his arrival, and woe betide me if I kept him waiting.

Bang on twelve-thirty, my phone pinged and, sure enough, it was Simon. I had my coat on ready to roll, and my bag to hand so I exited the house quickly.

I wasn't going to risk a punishment, as I had no clue what that might involve, and if I was tardy he might have second thoughts.

By the time, I reached the end of the path, Simon was standing there with the car door open, ready for me to enter.

Following the same routine as the previous evening, Simon made sure I was safely fastened into the car. He treated me like a princess, utterly considerate of my wants and needs. He then asked to see my lists, and I duly handed them over. He folded them, without looking, and placed them into the inside pocket of his dark blue jacket. His crisp white shirt, black jeans and black boots completed his outfit: smart-casual, but well turned out.

The journey took a little longer than last time, as the bistro we were having dinner at was almost in the centre of town. The bistro was called La Perla. The entire place was decked out in purple, silver and black, with the most amazing chandeliers. Enormous glass fish tanks separated the seating areas, and part of the stairway was also a fish tank of sorts. I was a bit frightened of standing on it in case the glass gave way, but this was obviously a specially made fish tank with toughened glass.

The lighting was quite low, and the smell of the food was piquant, making my mouth water.

The head waiter took our coats and led us to a secluded booth at the back of the restaurant. I shuffled in, and Simon slid in alongside of me. Our thighs touched intimately. Simon ordered some wine and then selected mains for both of us.

Drinks poured, Simon retrieved the lists I had given to him from his inside pocket and began to read them with interest, the expression on his face changing very little. He gave me no inklings to his thoughts, as to whether my desires were to his taste or not.

Finally, he said, "Well, my Pet, I believe there are numerous ideas that I can work with. Thank you, my Good Girl. Well done for compiling such a comprehensive list at short notice. Now, back to business."

With that, we went through my list, and a number of plans were made with regards to my training.

We were to spend part of the week getting to know each other better, and I was to learn the protocols and procedures, I would be expected to follow.

Nothing too complicated, but I made notes in any case.

The last thing I wanted to do was start off on the wrong foot and earn a punishment. Especially as I was clueless as to what said punishments might involve.

Thursday was to be our first actual play date. Meanwhile, we were going to visit Simon's home through the day, and possibly through to the evening, whilst I became accustomed to the positions I would be expected to learn.

The vast majority of the positions I already knew, and had used previously with Charles, and other Doms that I had played with in the past. Only a couple of the positions were new to me.

When at the house, I would wear a play collar and be naked at all times. I gulped at this one, as this wasn't

something I had done before. Totally naked, all day long? I had been naked in front of my Doms, especially when we played in private, but this was a big ask. I am a big girl, not quite a BBW, but not far off.

I just hoped the sight of me naked didn't stop the relationship dead in the water, and make him run screaming out the door.

Why do we always see our own faults, and not the good parts others see?

Like my bottom, for instance. Now that has always been in big demand, as apparently, it is very spankable.

Thank goodness for small mercies, or in my case fairly well padded, and nicely-shaped ones, to boot.

We chatted easily through the dinner and, with his natural dominance I had no problem remembering to be submissive.

As we finished off our dessert and ordered coffee, Simon said, "I would like to take you back to my house this afternoon, if you are willing, and trust me sufficiently, Little One? So, that we may begin your training and work out a way forward, including negotiations on a contract. This will be a written one ideally. But, if you prefer a verbal agreement will suffice. What do you think, Suzie?"

I didn't have to think this through for long. Over the short time I had known Simon, I had felt an electric connection but, most importantly, I felt safe in his company.

"Yes, Sir. I would love to see your home." I replied enthusiastically. I was eager to see where I might potentially be spending my Christmas holidays.

Simon smiled, then, his face lighting up and taking on a youthful look. I couldn't help but return his smile with my own.

"First of all, we have an important mission to accomplish. Come on, Little One."

Simon helped me into my coat, and we headed out the door, his hand on my lower back, guiding me.

Once installed back in the car, we set off down the road, and then we pulled into the car park of a local garden centre. I sat there, perplexed.

Simon opened the door and held out his hand. "I really need your help Little Miss, as this is the first time I have ever put up a Christmas tree in my home. I want you to help me choose a tree, and some decorations to dress it."

"I would love to help, Sir."

At home, my mum always chose the tree. Most of our decorations have a bit of history. Stuff I made at school when I was small. I used to love to dress the tree. I hadn't even thought about a tree and decorations in my little house.

He pulled me out of the car and held my hand as we walked toward the entrance.

As we stepped over the threshold, Simon laced his fingers through mine, making me feel safe and protected.

"First, we need to choose a tree. Then, we will have an idea of how many baubles and decorations we need."

"Yes, Sir. "I nodded. "First, though, are you thinking of buying a real tree, or an artificial one?"

"Hmmm. What would you choose, Suzie?"

"No contest, Sir. A real tree, please. I love the smell of evergreen, and the look of a real tree but it needs to be the kind that doesn't drop its needles."

Simon led me through the doors at the rear, into an outside area. There were trees of all shapes and sizes and an amazing smell of spices and pine surrounded us.

I inhaled. *God, I love the smell of a real Christmas tree*. I thought.

I turned in circles a few times, then saw just what I was looking for. Full and bushy, with a lovely shape. *We must have this one,* I thought to myself.

I tugged Simon after me, and took him over to the tree.

"This one, Sir. Please. I love it. It's just right. Not too big, and not too small and with lovely full branches."

"Calm down, Little One," he urged. "But yes, I can see what you mean."

He called over one of the assistants, who then carried the tree to a machine where it was wrapped in a net. He helped Simon to place it on a flatbed trolley with a basket attached.

"Happy now, Little One?"

"Thank you, Sir." I replied. "Very happy."

Now for the ornaments, I thought.

The assistant wrote Simon's name and address on a label, and we unclipped the basket from the trolley.

"Choose whatever you think we need, and don't hold back on the decorations, Little One. No expense spared, as I have none at home. "

We walked around and around the garden centre. Through the Christmas Grotto checking out all the made-up trees on display. The basket filled up quickly with baubles, ribbons and crackers. The final touch was a beautiful star, for the top of the tree.

I couldn't wait to get to Simon's house to set up the tree, and decorate it.

"Let me go and pay for these, and we can head to mine and set them up. I will order takeaway for dinner. Now calm down, Little One. Don't tire yourself out." He laughed.

The cashier promised to arrange for the delivery of the tree in an hours' time, and we placed all the decorations into the boot of the car.

CHAPTER 5

A s we headed to Simon's, it was obviously becoming colder, and frost was beginning to stretch across the landscape. The sky was now dark grey.

We pulled into a driveway off a quiet road. The houses were set back, affording privacy.

"Wow, Sir." I couldn't help observing. "This looks beautiful."

Not enormous, but obviously, the house of an executive of some sort or, as in this case, a hospital consultant. A sleek modern affair, with pale grey masonry, and granite steps leading up to a pair of large pillar box red double doors. It was approached by a wrap-around, tree-lined driveway, enabling cars the luxury of being able to pull in and pull out again with no problems. A separate garage was visible off to the left-hand side.

"Let me open up. Then you can assist me in bringing in our treasure trove," Simon said.

I waited by the car after Simon had helped me out, while he opened the doors. We gathered everything from the boot of the car, and headed inside.

An expansive hall was on view just beyond the doorway, with a traditional black-and-white tiled floor.

It took a couple of journeys back and forth to bring in the decorations, which we placed on a side table in the hall.

I slowly turned around, taking in my surroundings.

The hall opened out into a beautifully large space with a staircase in the centre. A corridor wrapped around behind. Two doors were either side of the hall and I could just glimpse a door at the rear of the staircase.

"You like, Little One?" He asked.

"It's gorgeous, Sir." I replied. "I love it. I think I expected something more modern, like the outside but this is lovely."

He glanced around. "Well I like it Little One. I am glad you like it too. Let's hang our coats up, and get a hot drink, shall we? Then I will show you the rest of the house."

With our coats safely stowed away, Simon led me to a large kitchen. It was through the door I had glimpsed behind the staircase. It was decorated in sunshine yellow with a large granite island unit shimmering in the lights. A welcoming Aga cooker was set on the left, in addition to a modern stainless-steel range cooker to the right. Altogether, it was an eclectic mix of old and new that seemed to meld together beautifully.

Two comfy wingback leather chairs were placed either side of a fireplace, looking inviting.

Simon walked over, and proceeded to light the fire, which was already prepared in the grate.

"Sit down there, Little One" He pointed to the chair on the left. "And I will put the kettle on. Coffee, tea, or maybe something else?"

"A cup of tea, please, Sir. I won't sleep tonight if I have any more coffee." I giggled.

I tucked my feet under me, and curled up in the chair. Two big cushions cocooned me in place.

I heard the kettle click off, and suddenly realised that I hadn't offered to help, so started to rise.

"Stay put, Little One. I've got this. I am an excellent chef, so a couple of cups of tea are no problem at all."

Does he have eyes in the back of his head? I thought, and found myself replying.

"Yes, Sir. Thank you, Sir."

We sat and chatted, drinking tea until the doorbell rang, and Simon rose.

"I expect that will be the tree."

I jumped up and followed him to the front door. Sure enough, a man was stood outside holding the tree.

Between the pair of them they wrestled the thing through the door, and then Simon indicated which room it was to go to. So, I moved ahead, as quick as I could, and opened the relevant door for them.

"Thank you, Little One." Simon said. "This way," he indicated to the delivery man. "Not far now."

The room stretched from the front to the back of the house, with a series of floor to ceiling glass doors at the rear. I could see a garden room beyond. I would have called it a conservatory, but, it was not the usual sort of thing I had seen before, as it had a proper roof.

It took my breath away. If I had thought the kitchen was gorgeous, I had no words to describe this room. The view through the windows and beyond was spectacular, with fields stretching out into the distance. I noticed that snow was beginning to fall, and drift softly to the ground. It was just a sprinkling so far, but the sky looked full of snow.

"It's snowing." I shouted.

Simon turned and said, "It's snowing, what? Little Miss?"

"It's snowing, Sir." I said, louder this time, and I felt my face heat up. What must the delivery man think? The tree was finally settled, in the far corner, in the distant left.

Simon showed the delivery man out, handing him a tip for his trouble.

On his return, Simon strode over to stand straight in front of me, and commanded. "Kneel."

Oh, shit, I thought. *Shit. Shit. Shit.* I dropped to my knees, assuming first position, my hands behind my head, tits pushed forward and my knees open for inspection.

I got too comfortable, and acted like a date instead of a submissive. What was I thinking? My thoughts raced.

"I thought you were an experienced submissive, and yet you forgot yourself so quickly. Explain yourself, sub?"

I felt myself filling up, tears brimming, ready to fall.

"So, sorry, Sir. I have only ever been submissive either in the bedroom, or, when playing in the bedroom. Although, I have always dreamed of a 24/7 relationship, I've never had one. I hadn't realised…"

"Stop. No. It's not your fault, it is I that should be sorry. I hadn't realised that was the case. You really should have told me, Little One. That does not excuse you, though, and a punishment will be forthcoming at the appropriate time. Now, the tree needs decorating. Where do we begin?"

I took a deep breath, and said, quietly, "Fairy lights, Sir. We start with the fairy lights."

Soon all the decorations were set out on the large coffee table, and the lights were twinkling on the tree. One by one the crackers and other ornaments were dotted about the tree. The only thing left to do was to top the tree, with the pretty star Simon had chosen.

He turned to me and said, "I think this is where we begin a tradition for the future, Little Miss." He took the star from its box, placing it gently into my hands.

"Be careful, it is quite delicate." With that he took me and lifted me up by my waist, as if I weighed nothing. He turned me to face the tree. I reached up, tentatively, and secured the gossamer, mother of pearl star into place.

"There now. Perfect." He sighed as he placed me back to earth.

My heart was hammering, and I felt my chest constrict. It was such a magical moment.

I looked around at all our hard work, and I could hear Simon move towards the door. He turned off the main lights with a click.

It was magical. The myriad of tiny white lights like stars, shone brightly, reflecting off the baubles and ornaments on the tree.

Simon pulled me back against him my back to his chest, as we both admired our work.

He pulled me closer, and I could feel his hard length against my back. My insides clenched, moisture pooling at my core. I wanted that hard length inside me. I jiggled, and rubbed my bottom against him. Feeling him grow, and harden in response. *Shit, his cock is so big.* I thought.

"Naughty little slut. You are a needy one, aren't you? But first things first. I have a punishment to administer, I believe."

With that he grabbed my hand, and pulled me over to the settee and across his lap. In a trice, he had my skirt flipped up and over my back, displaying my naked bottom.

"Now, that will be ten spanks for not remembering protocol and not calling me Sir. Ten spanks for topping from the bottom by rubbing against me, you naughty girl."

He rubbed my bottom, and I squirmed. "Stay still, or there will be more than twenty spanks, little slut."

Just as I was beginning to enjoy the feel of his hand on me, he raised it, and the crack of his hand on my bottom was explosive.

I shuddered, and tried to keep still. The burn spread quickly as each spank was added to the first.

I'm not sure when I began to cry but soon, big teardrops were trickling down and dripping onto the floor.

I lost count, and just tried my best to keep still. This Dom knew his stuff. My bottom was blazing, and my pussy was weeping.

Just as I thought it would never end, it did, Simon began to knead and caress my burning bottom, adding to the fire in my pussy. Both throbbing in time with each other.

I was so close to an orgasm: one touch in the right place would have sent me over the edge.

As if on cue, Simon bent close and whispered in my ear. "Come for me, Little One," and I exploded.

"Good girl. My Good Girl. That was so beautiful. Punishment is over, and all is forgiven. Now then, let's start how we mean to go on, especially as I believe someone is in need of a clean-up. The bathroom is across the hall, the one to the left. Remember the protocols and procedures we agreed. I expect you to return and strip naked in front of the tree. While you are in my home you will be naked at all times, except for when you are on a period, when I will allow you to wear panties. I am a Dom, and not an ogre after all."

Simon helped me to stand, albeit a little unsteadily. With that, he swiped his fingers through my folds, raising them to his lips and sucking them clean.

"Delicious, so sweet, my Little One."

I turned to head out of the room, and a slap landed on my rump.

"I couldn't resist. Now hurry up. The food will be here any minute and I have no qualms about letting you answer the door. If I think you are stalling. Naked, that is, Little One."

Oh, my God. Oh, my God. I do believe he means it. I thought.

I rushed out of the room, and down the hall in a flash. As I sat on the toilet, relieving myself, I thought through what had occurred so far since my arrival at Simon's. *Was I up to fulfilling my role as a submissive in real life? Although this had always been my dream. A power exchange, and my submission to a Dom. My Dom. Was I up to the task?* I wiped myself and then washed my hands quickly.

I need to hurry. If I am struggling with these basic tasks, how the hell will I get on answering the front door, to a total stranger, in the nude? I thought, worriedly.

As I rushed across the hall I heard the doorbell, and froze midway. My head swung automatically towards the outline of a figure, silhouetted in the window at the side of the door.

Simon appeared in the hall, tutting loudly as he approached.

"Oh, dear me. I did warn you Little One, didn't I? Now strip, and pass me the remainder of your clothing. Then you will walk serenely to the front door. Accept the takeaway delivery. Thank the driver nicely as you do. Do you understand, Little One?"

I stood, transfixed.

"Little one?" he queried.

Did I want this? If so I needed to obey, and complete the task. Chances are I would never see this delivery driver again. Could I do this? Could I submit, and so obey fully? Submit to Simon, absolutely?

Finally, with my decision made, I began to undress. Slowly at first. Then as Simon held out his hand impatiently, I removed my blouse, skirt, stockings, garter, and bra, as I undressed a little faster.

My heart was trying to beat its way out of my chest, and despite being naked I felt the first flush of my embarrassment. It began to spread from my face down to my chest.

I glanced up at Simon: his face was impassive. Waiting. Waiting, for me to obey him, or decide that this life wasn't for me, and walk away.

I gulped past the lump in my throat, turned and began what now felt like the longest journey to the front door. The delivery man, obviously grown impatient in the cold, rang the bell again. Then knocked loudly.

I found myself at the door. Tentatively, I reached up, and twisted the latch. Slowly, I opened the door.

CHAPTER 6

The blast of icy air and the blizzard, that seemed to hit me full on as I opened the door, took my breath away. My nipples hardened in response, to diamantine points. Goosebumps formed across my body and every little hair stood to attention. With eyes lowered, I pushed the door open.

All I could see of whoever stood at there was a very expensive pair of black shoes, and suit pants.

What the fuck? I thought. *Who delivers takeaway food dressed like that? This isn't the delivery man!* I realised my heart rate had just gone through the roof.

I was so humiliated and embarrassed that I simply couldn't raise my head up to see who it was.

The oddest thing was, that despite all this, and my heart rate ratcheting up so much, I thought I was going to explode. I felt my pussy gush, and could feel my juices begin to leak and trickle down my inner thigh. I clenched hard to try and halt the flow, but, all that managed to achieve was a further gush. Mortified, now, I couldn't move a muscle.

"Well, aren't you going to invite me in, Girl? I could freeze to death standing out here in this veritable snowstorm. Although I rather like the view. What a way to go." The stranger announced.

I shuffled backwards, awkwardly, trying to keep my thighs together, and heard Simon behind me as he answered. "Well, do as you are told, my Little One. Don't keep Alistair waiting, or our dinner will be stone cold." As I stepped back, Simon moved in and hugged the aforementioned Alistair, then took the many brown paper bags he was carrying from him. Alistair closed the door behind him.

"Meet my older brother Alistair, Little One. This is Suzie, the submissive I was telling you about. Come on through to the living room, near the fire, or my sweet submissive is going to die from hypothermia at this rate."

Alistair did no more than place his hand at the base of my spine and guide me, Dom style, into the living room and towards the open fire.

"Perhaps introductions are in order, Simon? I am Simon's older brother, as you may have gathered. Nice to meet you, Suzie." With that, he turned to me on the spot and formally shook my hand then proceeded to kiss me on both cheeks European style.

How freaky is all this? I thought.

"Did you know that research has shown that kink can run in families? We are both Dominants. In fact, I spotted Simon's potential and introduced him into the Lifestyle many moons ago. The amount of times that he got caught red handed, tying up his female buddies, was untrue. They put it down to his love of tying knots, having been a Scout, but I knew better by then."

"Sit, Little One," commanded Simon, and I sat gratefully on the rug in front of the fire, shivering violently.

I attempted to cover myself, as best I could, but knew that it was a pretty feeble attempt.

I could hear the pair of them chattering in the kitchen, and debated whether I should go and offer my help, but decided to stay exactly where I had been told to.

Soon, I could hear them crossing the hallway. The next minute a feast was being set out on the coffee table behind me. I hadn't realised I was that hungry, but then my tummy decided to second that and growled, audibly.

Both Simon and Alistair stopped their conversation, and turned to stare, then burst out laughing.

"Don't you feed your sub, Si?" Alistair quipped. "Bread and water diet, maybe?"

"Actually, we were out earlier having dinner but I hadn't realised how late it was. So, sorry, Little One. Your health and happiness mean a lot to me."

He walked over as he said this, and began to stroke my hair. I couldn't help but lean into him. *Much more of this, and I will begin to purr,* I thought.

Alistair, meanwhile, had returned to the kitchen to bring the last of the food, and a bottle of wine with three glasses.

"Dinner is served, M'lady," announced Alistair, as he bowed with a little flourish.

Simon picked up a plate, and handed it to me.

"Tuck in, Princess. You will need all the energy you can muster this week."

I waited until both Alistair and Simon had filled their plates, and stared at all the food. The table was laden with an array of dishes. Chicken breasts in some type of marinade, rice, chips, salad, and garlic bread. A real assortment. I settled on a chicken breast, salad, chips and a piece of garlic bread. My mouth watered, and I soon discovered it was all delicious.

Simon poured out three large glasses of merlot, and said. "A toast. To my gorgeous submissive. My Little One."

We raised our glasses, clinked them together, and drank. I hadn't forgotten I was naked, but somehow, as neither Simon nor Alistair referred to it, and concentrated on their food, it became less of an issue.

I asked permission to go to the toilet and, on my return, Simon and Alistair stopped talking. I had a feeling that I had been the topic of conversations.

Alistair was the first to speak. "Suzie, Simon said that you were supposed to be going home tonight, and stopping here over Christmas from Thursday, I believe. Unfortunately, I think you need to take a look outside."

With that he held out his hand and led me to the window at the rear of the house. I could see immediately that there might be a problem with my going home.

The garden, and beyond, was now covered in a thick blanket of snow. The reflection from the full moon made the landscape shimmer and I could see huge flakes of snow continuing to fall.

"Oh! But I have nothing with me, Sirs. No clothes, or toiletries. Nothing."

"That is no concern, Little One. Why would a naked submissive need clothes, in any case? We have a vast array of toiletries in the bathroom, as my mother insists that I have her favourites in case she wants to come and stay over with my father when they visit. Although, Mum and Dad are now very much aware of Alistair's Lifestyle and mine. So, usually, they choose to stop in a nearby hotel."

We all wandered back to the fireside and I picked a little at my food, then I enquired, "Do you see your mother and father over Christmas, Sirs?"

"Of course, we do. They are going to stop at Alistair's this time around, as currently he has no submissive. You will get to meet them over Christmas dinner, if you agree to move in. What about your family, Little One? Do you have a traditional Christmas dinner? Would you rather join your own family?"

"I hadn't thought that far ahead, Sir. I hadn't realised that you might want me to join you for Christmas dinner. Sometimes I go home for Christmas, but sometimes my parents go away. I'm not sure what they are doing this year."

"Well, we have enough time to sort who goes where. Maybe your family could join us here?"

I sat, thinking this through. *My family didn't know I was a submissive. What if Simon's parents said something?* I thought.

" Hey, don't worry about it. Why so sad? Mum and Dad are far too discreet to say anything about our Lifestyle choices. So, no need to worry, if that is the problem?" Simon said.

This allayed my fears somewhat. *Phew. Dodged that bullet*, I thought.

Alistair topped off our glasses, and fetched another bottle from the kitchen.

"Looks like you have two guests for the night, Si. No way am I going to risk that weather until it has settled down, and the roads are gritted. I didn't see a single gritter on the roads on my journey over. I think this has caught them by surprise."

"Where will I sleep tonight, Sir" I asked.

"In the Master bedroom with me, of course, Little One. I still need to give you the guided tour, don't I? Excuse us, Al. Al can see if there are any decent films to watch. No playing tonight, as we have all had far too much to drink. I will make some popcorn, and we will have a movie night."

Simon held his hand out to me, and I rose and went to him obediently.

"Good Girl." He whispered.

Those words. I thought, as I felt my pussy clench in response.

"Come my pet, let's get this over with. You already know where the bathroom, kitchen and garden room are downstairs. But, I am not sure you saw all of it, so let's start there."

He opened the door to the garden room and I could see the tree we had decorated earlier. I looked more closely at my surroundings, and took in the huge table situated at the far end of the room and twelve chairs sat around it. Two modern chandeliers sparkled above me. The room was modern and the colour scheme consisted of golds and creams. Two huge cream sofas set at right angles to one another, with a large coffee table in front.

I couldn't see a television anywhere in the room but a retro turntable and sound system was on display. The back wall held an extensive collection of vinyl records.

I walked over to the windows, and found I could hardly see the end of the garden, as the snow was falling so fast and thick. A veritable snowstorm, indeed.

Simon came over to stand behind me and said. "What a beautiful sight."

I replied, "Yes, Sir. It looks like a Christmas card outside, with the snow glittering and reflecting the light."

"Yes, that is beautiful, but I meant the sight of my gorgeous submissive girl, standing naked, framed by the snowy scene beyond."

"Thank you, Sir" I whispered. "You are too kind."

He moved closer, and I felt his warm breath on my neck; the heat from his body as he pressed kisses at the sweet spot on my shoulder, gently nipping my neck. Goosebumps arose afresh, and my nipples peaked as I let out a low groan.

"Hmmm. Little One, I can't wait to commence your training in earnest. To mark you as mine, my pet," he whispered. "Come. Let me show you the upstairs."

He flicked off the lights as we exited, and led the way up the staircase. His hand rested, once again, on the small of my back, guiding me.

The landing itself wrapped completely around the top of the staircase, with two lovely picture windows above the front entrance. Set either side, and between the windows, were built-in bookshelves with one of those fancy ladders attached to the nearest one, so that you could push it along and climb up to reach the books.

Window seats were built under both windows, matching the curtains that hung upstairs and down. Unlike the downstairs area, this one was carpeted.

Four doors were set about the upper floor, two to the rear and one to either side.

I had rushed over to take a closer look at the library, and heard Simon clear his throat.

"Did I say you could rush off like that, Little One? You need to be more mindful that it is my bidding you must do. Not merely follow your own desires."

I cast my eyes to the floor, and blushed a little, trying my best to look as contrite as I felt.

"So very sorry, Sir. I saw the library, and I love to read. So, forgot my place, Sir."

"I will let it go, this once, but make sure this sort of thing doesn't become a habit. We need to go over the protocols that I use, and discuss what I expect of you. I also need to know what you would expect from me, and any particular things you would be interested in attempting, "he said.

"Yes, Sir. Thank you, Sir."

He opened the door to the first room on the left, looking back from the library area.

"This is the room my mother and father sometimes use. Al will be using this one tonight, I imagine. All the rooms have *en suite* bathrooms, with a bath and shower in each."

The bedroom was spacious, with deep burgundy curtains and matching bedding. The bed was king sized, and a large, dark wood wardrobe lined the right-hand wall, opposite a picture window. Once again, a window seat and a small bookcase were positioned either side.

On the opposite side to the door was another door. I could see a lovely bathroom, with a white claw-foot bath, walk-in shower and two sinks. It was immaculate, with big white fluffy robes hanging on the back of the door. Towels were arranged in a large rack in the corner. Numerous toiletries were set out on a large shelf, which lay before two large mirrors over the sinks.

We didn't dilly-dally but, after a quick inspection, moved on to the next room. This one was facing the windows on the landing, and we entered the left-hand room first.

"Now, this room doubles up as both a dungeon, and a spare bedroom. Can you see why it would be both, Little One?"

I stepped into the room and looked around. At first, I was unable to notice anything untoward. Then I moved a little closer to the bed, and could see that the ornate bedhead had discreet rings attached at strategic points, to enable someone to spread-eagle an individual and tie them down.

I thought maybe the large landscape picture stood a little too proud into the room. Upon closer inspection, it proved to have almost invisible hinges. I easily pulled it open and, hidden behind it, was a narrow wall cabinet. Inside were a plethora of paddles, floggers, tawse, handcuffs and whips. Basically, everything a Dominant would need to play with, or punish, his submissive.

I closed the cupboard and turned to inspect the wardrobes. As I opened the first door I could see equipment hidden inside. A spanking bench, portable St Andrew's Cross, and another couple of mediaeval looking devices.

The drawers in the wardrobe looked innocent enough, until you opened them. Not so innocent, then.

They contained an unbelievable quantity and variation of sex toys. All manner of butt plugs, dildos of every shape, and size, and material. I could see a Hitachi, and a Doxy in there.

OMG, he has a Doxy, for goodness sakes, I thought. I clenched my thighs together as I felt a fresh gush from my core. *I squirt with a Hitachi; it will be a waterfall with a Doxy! Death by orgasm.* I thought, as I felt my pussy spasm, remembering my last experience with a Hitachi.

I hadn't heard Simon approach, so jumped when he said. "I see you have found something you like, Little One. I could see you clench from behind and saw the nectar that dribbled down your leg. Your perfume is overwhelming, and so sexy."

Although I love the experience of a Hitachi, I also dread it as I am utterly convinced that I am peeing when I squirt. Dominants seem to love a squirter, though. God bless them.

Once again, everything was closed, and you couldn't tell what you were looking at. This would look, for all the world, just like a spare bedroom, at a glance.

I had to smile, though, as the colour of the room and furnishings were red, and "Red room of pain" passed through my brain. So, Fifty Shades.

It was then that I noticed that there was a connecting door into the next room. Simon pushed it open and sure enough, there stood the Master bedroom, in all its glory.

This room was gorgeous. Shades of black, grey, silver, and mother of pearl shone from every surface.

A huge modern chandelier illuminated the room. It could have looked cold, but touches of colour stopped that from happening. Cushions of gold and bronze caught my eye.

A super king-sized bed took centre stage.

The bed I will be sleeping in tonight, with Simon, I thought. *Should I want to? Did I, though? Damned right I did.*

"Come, Little One. Let us view the final room, and return downstairs."

The last bedroom was another guest room, like the first but, whereas the first had burgundy accents, this one had a dark moss green.

CHAPTER 7

We returned to the living room, where Alistair was settled on one of the sofas with an enormous bowl of popcorn, and more wine poured into glasses on the coffee table. This was accompanied by numerous dips and chips.

"Is your pet happy to sit between us on the sofa, Si? Or will you have her kneel throughout the film?" He chuckled.

"I think I will allow her to sit on the sofa. What do you think, Pet?" Simon looked me straight in the eye as he made the last remark. Unsure how to respond, I stood there for a few minutes.

Alistair patted the spot next to him, and I was torn. *Sitting naked between two gorgeous Dominants might result in a very damp patch appearing under me,* I thought.

"I think she likes the idea, Si, but perhaps a soft blanket might help. Sitting naked on leather can have consequences. Sticking to the leather being one of them. Hmmm. Possibly other consequences too. Your pet's pupils are dilated, her nipples taut and a blush is on her cheeks and chest. I think your pet is aroused, and worried about leaving a puddle on the leather seating."

Simon turned me slightly and studied me.

Shit. shit, shit, I thought, as the blush proceeded to bloom on my cheeks, and elsewhere. *OMG, a dead giveaway that I am turned on. Are they both mind-readers? Is this another Domly trait?* I asked myself.

"I do believe you are right, Al. What do you say, Little One? Would you like a blanket to curl up on?"

I cleared my throat a little, unable to answer straight away. Finally, I managed to splutter "Yes, Sir. If I may, Sir."

Both Simon and Alistair chuckled darkly at my response, which clearly confirmed Alistair's observations.

As Simon disappeared to fetch a blanket, Alistair continued to study me. The hairs on my body stood on end in response, goose bumps pebbling my skin, and my pussy weeping in response to this treatment. I felt like a bug under a microscope, but a very turned-on bug.

The fact that Alistair didn't utter a word made me more nervous as I licked my now- dry lips.

Simon returned, and spread the blanket on the sofa next to Alistair, and patted it.

Like a good pet, I sat down as he settled in, next to me.

Using a state-of-the-art controller, Simon then proceeded to dim the lights before pressing play on Alistair's movie selection.

I had learned early on that Dominants could be very geeky. Cosplay and sci-fi were high on their lists of "likes". Simon and Alistair appeared to be no exception as "Guardians of the Galaxy 1" began to play.

As sci-fi, fantasy, cosplay and Steampunk are favourites of mine, too, I was a very happy bunny.

I sat there for a while, trying to decide what position to sit in. I was feeling uncomfortable sitting at the edge of the sofa, and more than a little exposed.

That was until Simon realised my predicament.

"What's wrong, Little One? Do you feel uncomfortable, being naked in our presence? Or is it Alistair's presence that is disturbing you? You seem to be very tense. So, tense that it is having an effect on me, too. "

"Sorry, Sir. I have only ever been naked in front the Doms I was play partners with, in the bedroom. The only exception being Charles, who wanted me naked in his presence at all times. But we only started playing a few weeks ago, and he had specific poses for me, and I was never allowed to sit on a sofa. What pose would you prefer, Sir?"

"We are not doing a scene, Little One, so no pose, thank you. I just want you to enjoy the film and be comfortable. But this is training, of a kind. You will become accustomed over time to being naked in my company. It will become second nature and of no consequence very soon. If we progress, as we should. I will want you to accompany me to an event in the New Year. Have you heard of CMnf? The initials stand for Clothed Male, naked female. As the name suggests, I wear a tuxedo and you, my sweet one, will be naked. That is, apart from what I allow you to wear. This could be stockings, a garter and heels, or nothing at all. In some respects, this should be easier for you, as you won't be the only submissive naked. All the submissive's present at this event will be naked."

I sat still while I absorbed this information. Rather than reassuring me, this new snippet of information had me worrying my bottom lip, nervously.

Naked! In front of a room full of strangers? Only stockings and a garter at most? Possibly not even that. I gulped as my thoughts ran away with me.

"Hmmm. Now then, Little One, is that trepidation? Or is it anticipation? There is only really one test of that, my sweet. Stand in front of me and assume the 'present' pose."

I didn't move one iota. I instantly realised that, despite my misgivings about such a scenario, I was dripping. Literally, dripping.

"Little One, are you disobeying me, already? Tut, tut. I feel she doth protest too much. Now stand," he commanded.

I stood, then moved clumsily to assume the present position in front of Simon. Legs spread, head up, hands behind my back with my chest pushed out.

Simon didn't move immediately but sat back, admiring the view, for a while. Out of the corner of my eye I could see Alistair, watching the scene with a serious expression on his face, as it continued to unfold.

Satisfied that I was presented appropriately, Simon reached over and slid his fingers through my folds.

My very wet, dripping, silky folds. My juices by that time had begun to slide unceremoniously down my inner thighs.

"Oh, Baby Girl. Exhibitionism? I didn't read that on your list, now, did I?"

He chuckled, loudly, and Alistair joined in.

Both now had huge smiles on their faces, and appeared to adjust themselves. Not discreetly, either.

Simon turned to Alistair, and stared at him for about a minute, and then turned back towards me.

What was that look all about? I wondered.

"Come on. Sit down, Little One. We have a film to watch, but, I think we need to have a little chat later on."

He patted the blanket next to him, and I returned to my place, leaning into Simon as I did. He pulled me closer, placing his arms around me.

I tried to watch the film but my mind kept returning to the earlier discussions, and that look between Simon and Alistair.

What was our little chat going to be about? The CMnf event, or something else? By the end of the film, as I watched the closing credits, I was a nervous wreck.

I excused myself to go to the loo, and as I sat, relieving myself, I felt a little odd. *What was going to happen next?*

When I returned to the living room, the atmosphere had changed.

Both men were chatting and stopped abruptly as I entered.

They turned as one and stood like twin statues, almost to attention, with their hands behind their backs, regarding me.

Unnerved, I moved forward, and then wasn't sure what to do next.

"Present. Kneeling, Little One." Simon growled.

I knelt quickly, legs parted, head up. Hands behind my head, pushing out my breasts and eyes lowered, as I'd been taught by Charles.

"Good Girl. Eyes up, Little One." Simon added.

I raised my eyes and looked toward Simon. He began to circle me, inspecting my posture, pushing my knees further apart with his foot. Then he pulled my hair back, exposing my taut, aching nipples. They stood to attention, as I craved his touch. My pussy was, once again, dripping. Being told I am a Good Girl always makes my insides clench and gush.

"Beautiful, my Little One. Oh, so beautiful." As he continued to inspect me intimately, he added, "Isn't she a beautiful pet, Alistair?"

I was aware, then, that Alistair was circling me as well, inspecting me closely.

"May I touch your pet, Simon? Would you mind if I touched you, Little One?"

I gulped, hard. I nodded briefly, acquiescing.

He crouched down in front of me, staring straight into my eyes as he proceeded to reach out, and I felt him cup my right breast. Weighing it with his palm, his thumb brushed over my sensitised nipple. I couldn't prevent my shudder, or the low moan he drew from me in response.

His eyes narrowed slightly as he raked a fingernail from my breast down across my ribs, trailing further, over the soft skin of my stomach, until finally he stopped at my hip.

I held my breath. I wanted him to carry on and touch my clit, give me the release I now needed. I felt my pussy throbbing, in anticipation of such a move, as I flexed forward in encouragement.

He tipped his head slightly to one side, as if he was weighing me up, which I was certain he was. He was watching every nuance.

He began to draw circles, trailing his nails over my skin, tantalising and teasing me. Tracing a path across my skin, lower and lower. Grazing and stimulating as he finally reached my apex, igniting a fire deep within me. He brushed up against my clit and I gasped out loud, biting my lip.

I was aware now that Simon was close by, watching every move Alistair made, and that every response of mine was being observed.

My breathing was now ragged. I could feel the heat of his breath near my face as he leaned closer.

I struggled to keep still. Quivering, I could feel the juices running freely down my inner thigh.

"Are you close, Little One?" Simon enquired, quietly.

I responded with a breathy moan. "Yes, Sir. Very close, Sir."

There was no use in my denying how close I was to coming. My body was already betraying me. My breasts were heavy, and aching to be touched. Hell, I could smell the musk on the air now, almost taste it. *One touch. Just one, and I will fall over the abyss.*

Juices trickled down from my sodden core. A sheen of moisture coated my upper lip, at the extreme effort it was taking to hold this position.

"May I, Si?" Was all Alistair said, and I could see Simon nod.

That signal was all it took, and Alistair plundered my swollen folds. My heart rate soared, heat spreading from my head downwards. My body was on fire. Breath hitched, as I got all religious, repeating, "Oh, my God. Oh, my God!" I shattered at his touch.

The waves of my orgasm crashed over me, drowning me in pleasure, as I squirmed and shuddered out my release. My legs were going to jelly, as I struggled to remain upright.

Alistair began to plunge two fingers deep inside. A frisson of heat and electricity made me arch and buck my body, as I continued to explode against his fingers. Mewling and gasping as the blood rushed in my ears, I closed my eyes, unable to keep them open, as stars exploded against my eyelids.

I parted my legs further, torn between wanting him to stop, and wanting more.

I was squirting over his fingers as he pumped into me, faster and faster. My pussy tightened once more as spasms racked my body. I tried in vain to pull away, but Simon had made his move. My back was against his chest, his arms holding me firmly in place.

Alistair moved forward, and knelt between my legs, preventing me from closing them, nudging them steadily farther apart. Opening me up for the final exquisite, yet excruciating, assault.

I splintered around his fingers; my final release. My juices were gushing freely to the floor as Alistair lapped at the fingers he removed from my apex.

Unable to keep my position, even supported as it was by Simon, my sated, boneless body continued to pulse incessantly with aftershocks, as Alistair finally removed his fingers. I heard him slurping my ample juices, and heard him mutter:

"Beautiful. That was so fucking beautiful. You taste so good, my pet. Fuck. I am ramrod hard, now. So, responsive. Thank you, my pet. Such a Good Girl."

Simon was cupping and stroking my breasts, and nibbling and sucking on my earlobes. Whispering in my ear.

"My very Good Girl. That was simply amazing. Such a gift to us both. Alistair and myself. "

I could feel how turned on Simon was, as his hard length pressed against my ass cheeks.

Alistair dragged his soft lips across mine. He bit my bottom lip, gifting me delicious pain. Licking the seam of my lip, he demanded that I open to him, and I tasted my essence on his tongue as I obeyed his unspoken command.

CHAPTER 8

I had died and gone to heaven, and was now becoming aroused afresh with all this attention: an overload of sensations, unlike anything I had ever experienced before.

Simon then whispered, urgently, in my ear, "Little One. Would you like us to take this further? Just say the word and we will stop, right now. But we would both like to take you. Have you ever been taken by two at once, my sweet? Are you willing to try?"

It took me a few moments to respond, as I was almost incoherent in my need. Adrenaline pumped through me as I managed to croak. "No, never done this before but YES. Fuck me, Sirs. I need you both inside me, now."

No sooner were the words out of my mouth than I was lifted and placed on the rug in front of the fire. Alistair continued to caress and fondle me, laving my adamantine nipples with his tongue, nipping and pinching, suckling and biting them as Simon swiftly undressed and sheathed himself. Unseen by me, he had also procured a large tube of lube.

Then it was Simon's turn to stimulate and pet me, as my honey continued to flow in anticipation. I was turned on in equal measure by the thoughts of the pain and pleasure to come.

I gazed up at my two lovers and groaned as I licked my lips in anticipation.

Fuck. What a magnificent pair they were. Looking at their cocks jutting proudly up, I began to realise what I was taking on. Neither of them came up short in the cock department. *I just hope to God that I can accommodate both at once*, I thought.

But which one would take which of my needy holes?

It was Simon who then growled out. "Your pussy is mine, Little One. Later, I will take that sweet ass. ALL your holes are mine. Every. Single. One."

With that, he crawled up my body and, with no more preamble, thrust into me with one almighty push. Plunging in that deep he hit my cervix, but was still not yet fully seated, balls-deep.

Fuck, he's big I thought. *Wide, too.* As I felt how tightly his cock fitted in my already ripe pussy.

Alistair knelt to one side, stroking his own cock in anticipation.

"I need to get deeper, Little one." Simon growled as he lifted my legs up and around my ears. Opening me up, as he began to plunge into me. His groans pushed passion higher.

"Oh Yes. Fuck. I can feel your pussy opening up for me and lengthening. In readiness for my cum."

As he continued to thrust, true enough, I began to stretch and accommodate his cock as it slowly plundered deeper, until I felt his balls begin to slap against me.

"Yes," he shouted." That's it. Now to change position, so that Alistair can prepare you, before I explode inside you. Alistair?"

"I'm here, bro, and almost over the edge, myself, watching you fuck our pet."

Simon rolled me over, and I felt a squirt of cold lube coat my rosebud as Alistair began to rim and play with my nether hole. Gradually, he started working in first one finger, then two until he finally opened me up. He stretched me, over a minute or so, then three fingers were inserted at once.

I began to fret a little, and resist worrying about being impaled by two huge cocks at once. Sensing my sudden reticence, Simon bit my neck at that sweet spot where the nape of my neck met my collarbone. He reached between us and brushed against my swollen, drenched clit as Alistair notched his cock again my bottom and pushed.

"Push back, my pet. Relax, and let me in," he gasped.

I pushed back, and felt my sphincter stretch and open, then he began to thrust, slowly at first. I felt the strange, but erotic, overfull sensation of both their cocks rubbing against each other through my inner walls.

Simon stayed still until Alistair was to the root, all the way into my ass.

The sensation of fullness was overwhelming. I hadn't realised I had been holding my breath until Simon commented. "Breathe, Little One. Here we go."

With that they began to slide in and out of my ass and pussy. I squirmed and quivered, overcome by the sensations and feeling of fullness.

"I am going to come, Sirs." I groaned and they both said.

"Come for me." They kept plunging into me as I crested the wave, and my pussy began to pulse and spasm around their growing cocks. Just as suddenly, they both shot their load into me. I could feel the heat of it, despite them both being sheathed.

They continued to thrust into me until completion as my body continued to throb and milk every last drop from them.

Finally, I was still, except for the pulses that occasionally beset me after coming so hard, which were making both sigh, and shudder in ecstasy.

Eventually, once flaccid, both pulled out and disappeared to dispose of the condoms and, presumably, clean themselves up.

I couldn't move an inch. A fine sheen of sweat covered my body. My hair was damp. My inner thighs and bottom were sticky from the sweat, cum and lube. Still. I lay there panting as my heartrate finally began to quiet and settle.

I think I would have nodded off, lying there in front of the fire, but it wasn't long before both Simon returned, Simon with a washcloth and towel, while Alistair carried bottles of water and a big box of chocolates. He grabbed the blanket I had sat upon earlier, as he passed the sofa.

Both kissed me tenderly, and then Simon gently began cleaning me with the warm washcloth, before patting me dry.

Once I was cleaned, Alistair raised my head, allowing me some sips of water. I hadn't realised just how thirsty I was, until I had quickly sunk half a bottle. He then placed some chocolate in my mouth.

As Charles had never given me any aftercare, ever, not in either private, or public, this made this all the sweeter. I felt loved and cared for.

Just as my eyelids began to droop, once again, I felt myself being lifted. The blanket was tucked around my limp body, as Simon easily carried me up to his bedroom.

My eyes closed as I drifted in and out of sleep. Alistair must have pulled the covers back as I was laid carefully into the bed, and I soon was sleeping soundly. Cocooned between two hot, firm bodies. My head on Simon's chest, Alistair's front to my back. Cradled by their arms. Safe and cared for.

CHAPTER 9

Morning arrived and I awoke to two pair of eyes contemplating me, to be greeted with, "good morning. Little One"

"Good morning, my pet."

I stretched, and yawned. Closed my eyes again for a few seconds. They were both grinning at me when I reopened them.

"Our little submissive looks so like a naughty kitten, when she yawns and stretches like that. Don't you think, Si?"

"Maybe food for thought? I do believe tails and pet play were on your curious list. Weren't they, Little One?"

My mind went blank for a moment, as I considered the implications of pet play. I had worn butt plugs before, but never an actual tail. It sounded quite exciting to me. I wondered if I could have ears too? I pondered.

"Hmm, it will depend on the weather, but I feel a little shopping trip may be in order but it depends on our Little One here, doesn't it? But, first, cleanliness is next to godliness, and all that. We will all shower and have breakfast. We have much to discuss."

Simon pulled back the covers, revealing that cleanliness wasn't the only thing on both of their minds. As the finest morning wood, I had ever beheld in my life greeted me.

I was pulled out of bed, and we trooped into the huge walk-in shower attached to the master bedroom.

It wasn't long before the shower was hot enough, and I was able to absorb more details about the bathroom.

Little details stood out, details which I hadn't noticed on my tour the previous evening.

The shower itself was a huge one. Very masculine, like the rest of the décor in the house. Granite style, dark-grey tiles bedecked the walls, and stainless-steel accessories gleamed.

The walk-in shower wasn't your usual empty space, upon closer inspection. Visible, set into the tiles, were stainless-steel rings, and a seat was on one side of the shower. An unusual accompaniment.

I fingered one of the rings, and Simon raised his eyebrows, saying. "Well spotted, Little One. There are numerous rings set into the walls in my bathroom. You never know when you might want to tie someone up and fuck them. The seat is very handy for some of my more inventive positions, and kinky Domly requirements." He wiggled his eyebrows a little, and I couldn't help but giggle at this comment.

He pulled me toward the multiple jets of water, and soon both him and Alistair were having fun, lathering up sponges and using their hands and fingers to clean my every orifice, until, once again I was a raging collection of hormones, and more than water and soap suds was dripping down my legs.

They produced condoms and lube and, after sheathing themselves, moved toward me with intent.

Alistair lifted my hands above my head, and I realised that Simon had procured a pair of stainless-steel handcuffs from somewhere close by. I was quickly secured to the steel tie above my head.

My heart rate ratcheted up a notch, and my breathing became ragged as he lifted me up and impaled me in one fell

swoop, pounding me against the wall. Goosebumps forming
on my skin as my back hit the cold unyielding surface.

I went to wrap my legs around his waist in an
automatic reaction until I was stopped by a command from
Simon. "No, Little One. How am I supposed to take what is
mine from behind, in that position?"

The next I knew, Alistair was against the wall and
Simon behind me, lubing my ass and stretching it in
preparation.

One, two then three fingers stretched and scissor my
hole, preparing me to take Simon's immense cock. Alistair
lifted me up by my ass cheeks, opening me up in readiness.

As I felt Simon's hot cock touch my rosebud, I
flinched a little, in anticipation of what was to come. Then,
remembering their instructions, I began to relax, and pushed
back. I was his, and I wanted him to take me. The ultimate
service: taboo, but erotic.

He pushed harder and the ring of muscles gave way,
allowing him entry. My bottom burned and stretched.

Pleasure and pain assailed my senses equally, each in
turn taking me higher. I wanted the pain and the pleasure.
Endorphins kicked in as he continued to push forward, and
Alistair began to move. Their cocks were rubbing against my
thin pussy walls, as I gasped and groaned.

Finally, fully seated to the root, Simon began to fuck
me. It was slow at first but, as one pulled out, the other
pushed in. The friction making my pussy weep. Hot juices
flowing freely amidst the water cascading over us.

It was a good job I was pinned between them. The
filling in their Dom sandwich, or otherwise I would have
plummeted to the floor.

Like wildfire through my veins and muscles I felt the approach of an immense orgasm beginning to coil through me. Every touch igniting my senses, as the heat flowed through my body.

I felt myself quicken, and both cocks grow as they approached their own release, as Simon commanded.

"Come for me, my Pet. Come for us." And I crashed over, screaming out and shouting incoherent nonsense.

They both continued to hammer into me. This was no gentle lovemaking. This was now feral fucking, as each made me theirs, marking me with bruises, as they bit my neck and breasts. I willingly let them mark me. Theirs. Then they both shouted out in unison.

"Mine."

Boneless, once more. I was impaled and they were savouring my flesh. Entwined as one. The sensations were intense, and our bodies continued to pulsate, long after all three of us had climaxed. Finally, the feelings ebbed away until they both withdrew, and, with kisses and caresses, told me what a Good Girl I was.

If Alistair hadn't caught me up in his strong arms, and I hadn't been attached to the wall tie with handcuffs, I would have fallen. They took it in turn to dispose of their condoms and, my handcuffs removed, I was set upon the seat as they washed me once again

They rubbed and inspected my wrists, checking my circulation and making sure I hadn't suffered any nerve damage.

Satisfied that I was cleaned to their exact specifications, I rose unsteadily but managed to make it to the sink where they both took turns in patting me dry, checking every crease, and crevice.

They even went so far as to apply body lotion, all over me, using long, sensuous strokes.

I was wrapped into a huge, fluffy, white dressing gown, and escorted back to the bedroom. I lay watching as they both dressed in jeans, black of course, and black t-shirts.

We made our way back downstairs, and I was bade sit at the island unit. Both men began to rustle up breakfast, refusing my help.

As they rattled the pots and pans, and set up the coffee maker I got up from my perch and wandered over to the window. The day was grey, wet, and miserable, with rain coming down in sheets. The snow of the previous evening was quickly being washed away. After the magical views of yesterday, it was a depressing sight. I stood there for a while, realising that I would have to return to my lonely flat later in the day. I felt arms encase me, and warm breath on my neck, followed by kisses and nibbles.

"Enough snow has gone, so that we will be able to take a trip to our favourite sex shop. Would you like that, Little One?"

"Yes, Sir. That would be lovely, Sir." I tried my best to sound happy at being able to travel somewhere, away from Simon's home.

"Now then, what's the problem, Kitten? You actually don't sound too excited at the prospect of a kitty outfit?"

I didn't want to sound ungrateful, but couldn't bring myself to answer.

"Come. Sit down. Breakfast is ready, and then we really need to have that conversation between ourselves." He indicated Alistair in this, as we headed back to sit at the island unit.

After a lovely full English breakfast of bacon, sausage, hash browns, beans, and egg, we relocated to the dining room, and sat at the table.

"Now, then, Little One." Simon began. "Originally, the arrangement I wanted was to have a Dom/sub relationship between you and me. But, after last night I want to offer you a slightly different arrangement."

Oh. Oh. I thought. *He just wants to be play partners now, after last night's antics.* I frowned, as he continued.

"Alistair and I had a little discussion yesterday, and wondered if you would be interested, and willing to consider, a relationship with both of us?"

I looked up at Alistair, who was nodding his assent.

"For you to be under consideration, for both of us. Well, what do you think, Little One? Is that a step too far for you? Taking on two Dominants, as opposed to one?"

My face lit up, and I couldn't help the huge grin that spread across it.

"I would love to be submissive to you both, Sirs. I have never experienced anything quite as mind-blowing as what we did last night. I feel connected to you both, and would be honoured to be under consideration to you both. Sirs. Thank you." I flushed, as tears of happiness slid down my cheeks.

We hugged and kissed, and decided to head out and visit the sex shop Simon had talked of earlier. We would choose a collar, to signify our new status, and check out the toys in anticipation of playing soon.

Dressed in my outfit from the previous day, I sat patiently, waiting for my new Sirs.

What a helter-skelter of a time I have had of late. I can't believe how quickly time has flown. Was it only yesterday that I was newly single? Now today, I have the prospect of not one, but two future Doms to serve.

CHAPTER 10

A decision was made to use Alistair's car, as it was on the driveway. All the snow had all but disappeared, except for a few patches in the fields, and on the hills in the distance.

The rain continued to fall steadily, the sky remaining grey and dismal. A complete contrast to my upbeat mood.

Before too long we arrived at the sex shop. The outside gave nothing away as to what kind of shop it was, with a shop front only showing lingerie and nice underwear. A sleek silver sign above the shop said "Sexy". Nothing more indicated the type of shop it was.

It wasn't a cheap sex shop, but very upmarket. With plush *chaises lounges* dotted around, and huge gilt-edged mirrors on the walls. Toys galore, with vibrators of every hue, shape and size, were on display in fancy glass cases. At the back of the shop was an extensive selection of kinky clothing: latex, leather and; lace.

A rack and some mannequins displayed a gorgeous selection of corsets, in every colour and size. Corsets were one of my favourite things.

Simon took my hand, and tugged me towards the display. Picking up various outfits, he began taking them and holding them up against me, with a quizzical look on his face.

"Stella. Can you give my beautiful Pet a hand choosing some outfits to try on? We will be attending any number of events over the holidays. You know Al's tastes, and mine, so you need to consider this. Suzie is under consideration to both of us. We will also need to try on some training collars, please."

Stella very quickly began to select outfits for me to try. Her arms full to the brim, she used her head to indicate where the cubicles were, and I headed over to an empty cubicle.

"Come on, Suzie, you lucky girl. Congratulations. Seems you are set to land two of my favourite Doms. You greedy girl. If you need any help with any of the outfits, just give me a shout. Leave the latex ones until last though, as they can be a devil to put on. I'll go and choose some more outfits."

Shocked at the sheer number of outfits hanging up in the changing room I faltered for a few minutes, unable to choose which I should try first. Then I heard Alistair's comment: "Come on, Pet. We are patient Doms, but even we have our limits."

I grabbed a corset and some underwear, and promptly dressed. Although, as I was nervous, it took a long time to fasten the fiddly metal clasps on the front.

I checked my reflection in the mirror, and stepped out.

Simon and Alistair were both sitting, nonchalantly, either end of a plush scarlet settee. Both sat bolt upright as I nervously approached them.

The wolf whistles they let out in stereo let me know in no uncertain terms that they approved of my choice. They leaned forward, for a closer look, then stood.

The corset was red and gold, with a tightly cinched waist and steampunk-styled clasps at the front, and laced up the back with black satin ribbons.

The panties were sheer, and black, but with red and gold embroidery.

"Present, standing." Simon commanded, and immediately I stood straighter, assuming the correct position.

Alistair and Simon circled my body. Like lions circling their prey. They sat back down and Alistair said. "Next outfit, Pet. Put that outfit to one side for purchase. Good Girl. You presented yourself well."

I beamed with pleasure, and felt my cheeks burn.

I weighed up my choices, and the next outfit was clearly another corset, but this time an under bust version. I checked through the various items of clothing hung before me, but couldn't see a blouse of any kind to put under it.

Just as I was about to check again, Stella returned. "Stella. Is there something else for me to put under this corset?"

Stella giggled, and dangled something up in front of my face and my mouth dropped open as I gasped.

She held up an intricate, but unmistakable item of both pain, and beauty. It was a pair of nipple clamps, with a chain between the two. Blue stones glittered as they twirled in her grasp

"The underwear to match these is here."

She pointed to a pair of panties, with a string of pearls where the gusset should have been. I picked them up shakily.

I dressed, nervous tension making the simplest tasks difficult. The corset in place, and wearing the underwear that now rubbed against my clit as I moved, I pinched my nipples in preparation for the next step. Pinching, and nipping them hard, I prepared them for the pretty, but lethal looking nipple clamps. Placing first one, then the other on my extended nipples, and leaving the chain dangling, I looked out of the cubicle and as I could only see my Doms sat waiting impatiently I stepped out. As before, I moved to stand in front of them, and assumed the standing present position.

It was then I realised we weren't alone in the shop. Stood at the counter, being served and handing over a lethal-looking bullwhip to be wrapped, was a familiar face... Charles.

I startled, and was just about to turn tail and walk back to the cubicle, when he turned and spotted me.

It could only have been a few seconds, but time appeared to stand still. One minute became ten. Transfixed in terror, which must have shown on my face, I became aware of Simon and Alistair turning around to see what, or who, had frightened their sub so much.

The soft music that had been playing in the background faded away. Blood rushed through my ears, as the tumultuous thoughts in my brain overcame my mind.

Fuck. Fuck... What the fuck? Of all the places for Charles to be! Here? Now? I thought.

My arms automatically wrapped around myself, as I took a step back.

Charles slammed the bullwhip onto the counter.

Eyes narrowed, tendons standing out on his neck he turned hurriedly. His expression hardened. First, he took one step closer, displaying confusion, then realisation set in as he stabbed a finger towards me.

"You... Where. Have. You. Been?" Charles roared.

The veins throbbed in his neck. His jaw clenched. His hard, glittering eyes were taking in the scene.

A flashback hit me. The knot in my stomach grew, as sweat beaded my upper lip. I rubbed my cold clammy hands up my arms, as the charged atmosphere encompassed the room.

Then Charles stopped, as he and I both realised that, this time, I wasn't alone.

This time Simon and Alistair were here, and seeing my strained appearance, had begun to rise as one, to face Charles.

Simon spoke first. "Good evening Charles. I don't believe you have had the pleasure of meeting my brother, Alistair. He inclined his head toward Alistair, turned and said to Alistair. "This is Suzie's ex Dom." Emphasising the ex. "I told you how I met Suzie at the club, and under what circumstances."

Then he directed a comment to Charles. "Suzie is now under consideration to both myself and Alistair."

Charles stepped back, as if in shock. Then looked from one to another of us with disdain.

"Sorry, Simon. I was unaware of Suzie's change of status." He forced the words out between clenched teeth. With that he turned and moved back to the counter, and in hushed tones completed his purchase.

Crisis over? I asked myself. *That was easier than I thought it was going to be. But, then again what chance did he have with both my future Doms in the room.*

I watched him leave, and realised I was shaking with the after-effects of the confrontation that didn't quite happen.

Simon and Alistair fussed over me, and Stella brought me a glass of water. Once I had recovered sufficiently, I continued my catwalk show for my Doms, although all my excitement had dissipated. Then I re-dressed in my own clothes. With our goodbyes said to Stella, we began to leave.

I suddenly felt drained, once I found myself in the car. I must have dozed off on the way back to Simon's house, as

I was jolted awake by being lifted out of the car. The cold damp air hit me full on. It was still a miserable day.

I snuggled closer to the warmth of whoever was carrying me, then Simon's scent let me know who that was.

As we entered the warmth of the house, I murmured "Thank you, Sir," as I struggled to detach myself from his arms, but Simon was having none of it.

"Behave, Little One. You need to rest, so back to bed for you for now. I believe a powernap is in order. Doctor knows best. You had a pretty traumatic experience earlier. I could feel the tension in your body. Rigid muscles, and the way you played with your hair showed me how much that episode affected you. Alistair and I will order food in, and we will eat once you have napped."

"Yes, Sir." I acquiesced, forcing a smile. I was too tired to argue at this point.

"Good Girl," he responded. The next thing I knew, I was tucked up back in bed and I fell quickly asleep, exhausted.

I awoke about forty minutes later far from rested, but no longer able to sleep. My brain continued to work overtime.

As I entered the living room the low sounds of conversation stopped, I stood in the doorway.

"Little One, come here and present yourself. We would like to see what you look like wearing your collar of consideration."

On the coffee table, set out, were many of the items bought earlier, including a lovely teal leather collar. On the front was a stainless-steel ring.

I approached, and knelt as Simon reached over to finger the collar.

"It may be a little stiff, initially, but don't worry, we will oil it to soften the leather. The only marks you will wear will be intentional ones, from when you are naughty. They will signify who you belong to, my Pet."

Simon then knelt to one side of me, and Alistair the other. Alistair lifted my hair, as Simon slipped the collar into place, fastening the buckle and tightening it so that it fit snug around my neck.

Both stood, and bade me "Stand, Little One."

I went into the present position immediately, and lifted my head, eyes lowered.

"That colour certainly suits you, my Pet," said Alistair, as Simon circled me.

"Yes. A lovely addition, and it contrasts so well with your fair complexion." Alistair continued.

"Thank you, Sirs. I am honoured to wear your collar. May I see it in the mirror, please, Sirs?"

"Of course, you can, my Pet. Go and see what you think."

I turned to the big mirror over the fireplace, tentatively touching my new collar. It was a little stiff, but the colour was beautiful, and I was proud as punch to wear it.

"Now then, we have ordered a variety of Chinese dishes for supper and, unless you want to experience your first punishment for disobedience, I suggest you remove all that you are wearing, apart from the collar. You do remember our instructions. Don't you?" Simon teased.

"So, sorry, Sir. I was so distracted that I forgot that I was meant to be naked, unless instructed otherwise."

I fumbled with my clothing and quickly rectified the situation, placing my clothes neatly in a pile on one of the chairs.

Once again, I could sit between my two Doms as we watched catch-up TV: An episode of Game of Thrones.

I watched, fairly contented, as they fingered the toys set out on the table: butt plugs of varying sizes. Inflatable toys, and numerous other items such as clover clamps, floggers and paddles. As if this action wasn't out of the ordinary.

The doorbell rang, and Simon answered while I helped Alistair place the toys back into the carrier bag.

I tried to put the incident with Charles to the back of my mind, but lost the thread of the conversation, several times. My thoughts were turning inwards.

CHAPTER II

I ate, distractedly at first but, with all this new-found attention, I eventually rallied as the evening continued. I thought my Sirs would be itching to play, but all that occurred was a fresh bout of love-making once we were all ensconced in the master bedroom.

Sitting, watching my Sirs play with the new selection of toys had taken its toll on me. They hadn't failed to notice the decidedly soggy patch on my blanket.

Soon we were all back in the master bedroom. My Sirs were still fully clothed and I was still naked.

I was instructed to kneel on the bed, doggy style. The carrier bag was emptied out, and I could feel my nectar running down my inner thighs. Anticipation increased as I waited to see what toy would be used first. I didn't have to wait long, as I felt the first cold squirt of lube hit my bottom. I let out a gasp as first one finger, then two were inserted to the knuckle and my anus was stretched in readiness.

I could tell by the cold, hard sensation that it was the huge glass butt plug that was being eased into me with the command.

"Push back and let me in, Pet. Let's see if we can achieve a nice gape with this one. Hmmm. Bigger than you have had before, my Pet."

I nodded, then remembered to add, "Yes, Sir. Much bigger." I acknowledged as I groaned loudly.

Simon had decided that a DP session with the toys was in order. I felt him sweep his fingers through my sopping folds and push a dildo into me with ease.

I closed my eyes and moved slightly, pushing backwards and forwards until I was rewarded with a spank.

"Did we say you could move? Little One? Stay still, until we tell you otherwise," Simon admonished.

The butt plug now fully inserted, Alistair took over, thrusting the dildo in deeper and deeper, making wet, squishy noises.

"Greedy girl. So, fucking wet and needy. Aren't we?"

"Yes, Sir"

Just as I was beginning to feel the start of heat moving down my body, my face flushing as an orgasm was quickly approaching, I felt the first hit of the paddle.

Caught off guard I moved a little and was thwacked again on the other cheek.

My orgasm was approaching faster now. The heat of my bottom matched the heat generated by my head, and down my chest.

"Come for me, Pet?" Alistair instructed.

I needed no further encouragement, as my orgasm swept through me, as I screamed out my release.

"Keep your position, Little One. Did we tell you to move, or lie down?"

They continued to paddle my bottom with vigour as they pumped the butt plug pulled in and out. Ecstasy and agony. Pleasure and pain. A heady mix.

Finally, they relented, and Alistair instructed., "There you go, Pet. We will give you a few minutes to recover," as the butt plug was gently pulled out.

"Well, Simon? What do you think of the lovely gape our Pet is displaying for us? I think she is ready for round two. Don't you?"

No further encouragement was needed, as they both stripped in quick order, sheathing themselves

This time, though, Alistair lay down and pulled me over to him, pushing inside me easily, as Simon climbed on top and just as easily entered me from behind. My gaping bottom allowed his easy access.

This was not to be a gentle coupling, or whatever you call it when three people are involved.

Simon held his full weight off me as Alistair pushed up and down, hitting bottom every time. I relished the feel of their ample girths rubbing through the walls of my pussy.

The orgasm that blasted through me caught me unawares as my pussy pulsed around them. Less than a minute later the heat of them entering me, allowed a second that prompted a rolling orgasm of my own.

Once our bodies had quietened, we lay sated and sweaty for a while until it was a little uncomfortable.

Then came a lovely shower where I was spoiled rotten by my Sirs as they petted and preened me, taking care to clean every inch, more than once.

It was only Tuesday, and so much had happened, already, I thought as I drifted off.

The next morning, I awoke before either of them, and spent some time watching them sleep. They were different, but also had so many similarities.

I was watching Simon when I realised that Alistair was awake, and watching me watching Simon.

"Enjoying the view, my Pet?"

I smiled in response. "Yes, Sir. It is such a lovely view. Waking up to two gorgeous Doms."

He snuggled up to me, and I felt his very hard, long, length nudge my back. "Hmm. What a gorgeous sight, first thing in the morning," he murmured as he pulled the covers down a little. My nipples hardened at the cooler air of the bedroom.

He leaned over and tweaked first one nipple, and then the other. Hard.

"Turn to me, my Pet. I want to taste you."

I turned, and his mouth encompassed my right nipple. He nibbled and sucked: first one, then the other. As he pulled me toward him, his cock notched at my core. I was lifted up and, the next thing I knew, I was impaled. As he pushed into me, stretching me, I caught my breath

Jesus, he's big. I began to open, to accommodate him. He didn't move much, just gazed into my eyes as he stilled.

"How's that, my Pet? So, hot and wet. So, tight around my cock. I am sure we will both be so happy when we can dispense with these condoms." He began to move slowly. His cockhead hit my cervix with each thrust as I stretched around him.

"Holy fuck. You feel so good, Pet."

I began to move with him, as I felt another pair of hands begin to stroke my bottom. Simon was awake, obviously, and equally aroused.

"You started without me, Al. You always were a selfish prick," he quipped.

I heard the bedside drawer open, and close. Then the unmistakable sound of lube being pumped.

I looked to my left, and Simon kissed me deeply as I felt cold lube being liberally applied to my bottom.

No guessing what would happen next, as Simon deepened the kiss and pushed two fingers into me.

Scissoring and stretching once more. Another finger entered my nether hole as Alistair continued to pump into me.

"I am so happy to see that you are able to stretch a bit more each time, my Little One. We will begin your anal training in earnest, soon."

Alistair grabbed my bottom and pulled the cheeks wide, opening me up even further.

"Come and join the fun, Si, or I will shoot my load before you even get started."

Alistair flipped over, taking me with him and I was suddenly on top.

Simon pushed against the muscles of my sphincter, then he was inside me.

A slight burn this time, then that overfull feeling, as they both picked up the pace.

Each session with them both entering me was becoming easier.

Once again sensory overload began as first one, then the other, plunged into me. Their hard lengths pushing against each other through the walls of my pussy.

Heat began in my head, then throughout my body as my climax swiftly approached.

I felt a tightening in my tailbone as heat suffused my entire body. Pulse, after pulse, beset my body as first Simon, then Alistair emptied into me. The grunting continued as they carried on until they both stilled, spent. Our bodies continued to twitch and spasm.

Hot and sweaty as we were, we stayed in this position for a few minutes, spooning, until Alistair recovered and they both shifted around to lie either side of me. We drifted back off to sleep again. I had never felt more wanted, or safe as I did in their arms. Thoughts of Charles faded away.

When I awoke, I lay there quietly wondering whether I would be allowed home today, as I really needed to get myself organised.

Despite having a break over Christmas, I had assignments that I needed to research, and all my text books were at home. I needed to make a list, as my laptop and various other items were necessary if I was to keep up and pass my next assessments.

I also needed to pick up a fresh supply of the pill. The last thing I needed, right now, was the patter of tiny feet.

I woke and stretched slightly; both Doms still slept soundly. Each still holding me close sandwiched between them.

I needed the bathroom, desperately. I managed to wriggle out, and quickly rushed across to the bathroom. I shut the door behind me softly, so as not to wake my two sleeping beauties.

I forgot, in my haste to empty my bladder, that this was a forbidden act. One of the rules I had been given involved leaving the door open at all times.

I washed my hands and looked into the mirror, finger-combing my messy bedhead before attempting to open the door quietly once more.

Unfortunately for me, two pairs of eyes fixed onto me as I tried to sneak back into the bedroom.

Oh dear, I thought. *What's with those unsmiling faces and raised eyebrows?*

Alistair raised himself up onto his elbow, and spoke first. "Now then, Pet. Do you remember the rules you were given when you first came here?"

I stopped, flummoxed, trying to remember what I had agreed to. Being naked at all times, was one, and I tried in vain to remember the others, until the penny dropped. Quite literally.

Oh. Shit, I shut the door when I went into the bathroom to pee. Stupid girl Suzie! I admonished myself, in my head.

"Sorry, Sirs. I was trying to let you both sleep."

"Kneel. Little One." Simon commanded, and I fell to my knees, my eyes lowered in shame.

"I would spank you, Little One. But that would really be a pleasure for you, as I remember how wet you got when I spanked you. So, if Alistair agrees, I think some corner time is required. Don't you think so, Al?"

Alistair nodded his agreement and added. "Pet, you can sit in the corner of the living room quietly without moving for fifteen minutes after breakfast. I expect you to hold your position, with your nose to the corner."

With my eyes still lowered, I heard the bed creak slightly as they both got up and left the bed, Simon heading into the bathroom, as Alistair began to don his clothes. Once both were dressed and had gathered their belongings I was allowed to descend with them to the kitchen, but bade kneel as each busied themselves.

Simon started making omelettes, and Alistair poured glasses of orange juice for the three of us and put on the coffee machine.

I could sit at the breakfast bar to eat, but neither of them spoke to me directly. They continued to chat to each other, as If I wasn't there, but invisible.

My cheeks heated in shame, and by the time breakfast was over and the pots cleared away I had unshed tears in my eyes. I walked obediently to the corner of the living room, and did as instructed.

Would my two Doms still want me when I couldn't even follow the simplest of instructions? I pondered.

CHAPTER 12

I knelt, with my nose touching the wall. What seemed to be a simple task got harder by the minute. For one, I really needed to scratch my nose. Why is it that when you are not allowed to do something, that is the one thing that you find yourself wanting to do? I was even tempted to rub my nose on the wall, to ease the itch in my frustration but continued to do as instructed.

After what felt like hours, I finally heard both my Doms approach quietly.

"Rise, Little One." Simon instructed, and then I was enveloped in two strong pairs of arms. Encased, as both Doms kissed and petted me, and repeated over, and over.

"What a Good Girl, "and "My Good Girl" and my tears, that I had held back until now began to fall.

"Hey. Aww. Pet. What's the matter? Once a punishment is over all is forgiven and forgotten. That is part of the equation of Dom/sub. Surely you knew that?" Alistair crooned.

Between sobs I managed to finally splutter out. "Charles would give me the silent treatment for a while after a punishment. I wasn't sure what to expect…"

Both hugged me tighter, leaving me feeling treasured and protected, and I realised that this is what a true Dominant and submissive relationship should be like. Not the mean-spirited treatment I had received from Charles.

My sobs subsided, and I was thoroughly kissed by both men until I started to giggle and got a playful swat on the bottom.

"Now then. "Simon said. "I do believe that, as it is a beautiful sunny, but cold day outside, maybe you would like to go home, and sort out what you would like to bring on Thursday. Both Al and I have arrangements to make later today, so you will stop at home tonight. One of us will come and pick you up tomorrow evening. What do you think, Little One? Can you manage one night without us?"

I beamed back, "Yes, Sirs. I have a lot to sort out at home. I need to water my plants, and write some Christmas cards. I also need to do a little Christmas shopping, if I can fit it in."

"Don't worry about the shopping. Al and I thought maybe we could all visit the Christmas markets together, and do some shopping at the weekend. If it pleases you?"

"That sounds wonderful, Sirs." With that, I was despatched upstairs to dress, and gather my belongings. It was going to feel strange being at home on my own. Maybe Claire could come around, and have some supper? We could watch some chick flicks.

Alistair was given the task of driving me home, as Simon had a few private patients to attend to that afternoon.

I said my goodbyes to Simon, with long, lingering kisses. Then waved him off prior to Alistair indicating that we needed to head out.

He insisted on opening the passenger door, and making sure I was comfortable before heading back to my home.

Alistair told me a little more about himself, which was great, as I wasn't too sure about asking him any questions.

He was a solicitor, and a senior partner in a prestigious local firm, Harvey and Pallett. Soon, we were pulling up in front of my house.

He made sure the house was safe and secure, and didn't leave until he was happy that I was settled.

We shared long, lingering kisses and hugs, accompanied by innuendo concerning what himself and Simon would be doing to me at our next meeting.

My first job was to check the fridge, and see what food I had left. Not much, to be honest, but enough milk for several cups of tea, and I knew I would be able to throw something together for supper. Maybe a couple of tins of tuna and some dried pasta. Staple diet of university students everywhere. I even managed to find half a garlic bread in my little freezer compartment.

Bingo! That was supper sorted for tonight

Brew in hand I sent a quick text to Claire, offering supper, a bottle of wine and a catch-up.

It wasn't long before I got a reply.

Abso-bloody-lutely. I want to know all the dirty details of your time with Simon. What time? I have a bottle of red I can bring.

A bottle each seems like a plan, I think.

I sent back.

How about 7pm? We can make a night of it. With supper and a chick flick.

Game on, see you at 7, came the reply.

I fluttered around the house as I tidied up, putting on my washer, and setting to, to make supper.

By the time it was seven o'clock, supper was ready to roll. Two glasses were laid out on my little coffee table in front of the telly. Red wine poured, left to breathe, and the aroma of garlic bread filled the air.

A knock at the door heralded Claire's arrival. After hugs and air kisses, we were soon set up on the settee. A throw over our knees. A plate of tuna pasta with a slice of garlic bread on the side of the plate.

We settled on one of our favourite films, ***Coyote Ugly***, and sat back. Fork in one hand, wine glass in the other. About ten minutes in, Claire simply couldn't wait any longer and grabbed the remote and paused the film.

"If you don't bring me up to speed about your dirty doings this week, I will simply explode," she said.

I couldn't help but smile, and started to describe all that happened over the last few days, in detail. Including the scary episode with Charles.

We chatted, and after I had told Claire every dirty little detail, we continued with our film, joining in with the songs as per usual.

Finally, all the wine drunk, and the bowls and plates now soaking in the sink, we found a couple of miniature whiskeys (a remnant from a weekend abroad) and finished the evening with an Irish coffee each. Chatting about what plans we both had for over Christmas, and agreeing to meet up for a few drinks when we could.

I told Claire about my commitment to stay with Simon and Alistair over Christmas, and she thought it sounded like a great idea. Especially, considering the way Charles had acted in the sex shop.

"OMG. How lucky are you. Not just one gorgeous Dom. Oh, no, you manage to bag yourself a pair of the buggers. I need to find myself a nice Dom. Do they have any more brothers waiting in the wings?"

We both burst out laughing at that. "Sorry, Claire. Don't think they have another brother, but I can ask."

Soon we were both yawning. A combination of wine, food etc.

"Let's head to bed. We can chin-wag until one of us falls asleep." I said.

The chin-wagging didn't last very long, as we were both asleep almost as soon as our heads hit the pillows.

CHAPTER 13

We surfaced the next morning about eleven, furry tongued, and in need of plenty of fluids.

"I brought you a cuppa tea. Would you like a bacon buttie?" I said.

"Not half. Hmm, just what I needed. Breakfast in bed?"

"Why not? Sounds like a plan." With that I fried up some bacon, and used the last of the bread, as well as making a fresh pot of tea, to top up our mugs.

"This is the life, Suzie. Shame we can't do this more often." I said, as we sat in bed enjoying our breakfast.

"Have you heard where our next placements will be? I'm hoping it's more exciting than outpatients." I said.

"No, not seen anything posted yet. We could nip into Uni later, if you like? Might go up on the noticeboard before going online. I have some books to return to the library, otherwise I will need a bank loan to pay my fines." Claire chuckled.

"Yeah, I know what you mean. I have a couple I need to renew but I think I can do them online."

"Come on. Let's clean up the pots and head over. We can have another cuppa in the canteen."

Wrapped up warm against the bitterly cold weather, we both climbed into Claire's little red and white Mini Cooper. We parked up at Uni, making sure to put a parking ticket on the car. Once my books were returned and I had picked up a book that I had ordered, we nipped into the little café on campus. I treated myself, and Claire, to deluxe hot chocolate drinks, topped with little marshmallows and whipped cream.

By the time, Clair had dropped me back at my place dusk had fallen and frost was forming on the grass.

I made way inside and flicked the heating on. Before long my little house was cosy and warm.

I had forgotten to call for anymore shopping, so was deciding whether to head out back to the little corner shop, or go and place an order with the nearest supermarket that delivered.

Just as I was debating this my mobile rang.

I picked it up and could see *mum*, so answered straight away.

"Hi, Mum. How are you?" I asked.

"I am doing great, Suzie. Just thought I would see what you are up to over Christmas, and New Year. Have you got any plans? Darling?"

"Why? What's happening? I thought you and Dad would be going on a cruise as per usual?"

"We decided not to bother with a cruise this year," she replied.

"Oh, bugger." I said. "I've already made some plans for over Christmas, but I am sure I can swing by and see you both."

"We thought maybe we could see you Christmas day?" Mum said, sadly.

"Can I get back to you, mum? Just need to check what arrangements have been made. Love you. Can let you know my plans later today. At the latest tomorrow. Bye for now."

"Bye, Lamb. Love you too. Speak soon."

Torn, now. *What should I do? I have already agreed to be at Simon's, with him and Alistair. He mentioned*

Christmas dinner with his family, didn't he? I know he said his family is understanding, but what would my mum and dad make of all this? Bugger. I need to think. Shit. I also need to pack some clothes and stuff to get ready. Good job we agreed to change the day to Friday, I thought.

I had messaged Simon the previous evening to change the plans, and I was now being picked up Friday evening.

I set about hunting down several outfits, with no idea what I would need. As they expected me naked through the day and night, I was clueless. So probably packed way too many outfits.

Time flew, as I rushed around, in order to be ready on time. I needed to shower, shave and do my hair. Maybe even paint my nails.

Everything packed up ready to roll, I sat back and relaxed with a cup of green tea and a slightly stale biscuit. Nails drying, with half an hour to spare. Phew.

Just then my doorbell rang, and I shuffled to the door, toe separators flapping crazily.

Who could this be? I thought.

I opened the door, and a guy stood there, a dark-haired chap I didn't recognise at all.

"Taxi for Suzie?" He said.

"Sorry." I replied. "I've not ordered a taxi. Not sure how you got my name and address."

He flashed his taxi badge, and continued. "A gentleman called Simon booked this for you. Something about car problems? Said you were to come with me, and I would take you back to his place. He said someone would be there to let you in."

I stood there, puzzled, for a few minutes, wondering if I should ring Simon and check this out. But, realistically, what were the odds of a taxi driver turning up at my door knowing mine and Simon's plans, and my name?

"Just give me a few minutes to put my boots, and coat on. Luckily, I am all packed and ready to go."

I took one final swig of my drink. Nails now dry, I put my socks, boots, and coat on, checked the windows and doors, and headed out. The taxi driver insisted on carrying my bag to the car.

I looked to the curb, and sure enough a cab was parked there, hazards flashing. Soon I was ensconced in the back-seat. Butterflies began in my stomach as we slowly pulled out into the stream of traffic.

I sent Claire a quick text letting her know I was on my way to Simon's, saying I would let her know once I arrived there safely. I explained about the change of plan, and that a taxi had arrived to pick me up half an hour earlier than originally planned.

Roger that. Claire responded. ***Safe journey babe Xx***

I settled back and watched the Christmas shoppers out and about around town as we travelled up the road.

I was feeling a little off-kilter. Twice, now, we had turned in the wrong direction.

"Where are we going, exactly?" I asked.

"To the drop off point I was given, Miss."

"Pull over. Pull over now. This is the wrong direction. I need to speak to Simon, and find out exactly what is going on," I insisted.

I heard the locks click on immediately. I tried the door handle, despite the fact that we were still moving.

"Stop the fucking car, right now! What the hell is going on?" I screamed.

He didn't reply. Nothing. He just stared straight ahead, so I reached for my phone to call Simon.

It went straight to voicemail.

"Simon, it's Suzie. Where is this taxi driver taking me please? I thought I was coming to your place but now we are right over the other side of London. And he won't speak to me. He has also locked the doors. I am getting very unnerved by all this. Please ring me back as soon as you can."

I sat there, staring out of the window for a few minutes, trying to work out what direction we were heading in, but as there were no landmarks I recognised, I was unsure where we were.

Suddenly, my phone rang. I could see the caller was Simon, so answered straight away.

"Hey, Suzie. What's going on? Neither myself nor Alistair ordered a taxi to pick you up. The arrangements stand. Al was picking you up. What did this guy say exactly?"

"Something about car trouble, and that you had rung and booked a taxi to pick me up. But we are going in the wrong direction for your place." I felt sick, now, and my heart was racing.

"Suzie. My pet. Get out of the cab now. This instant. Tell him to pull over, and let you out. Work out where you are, and Alistair will come for you." He was using his Dom voice, but sounded strained.

"I asked him to pull over, and he has just been ignoring me ever since. The most worrying thing is that he has locked the doors. I couldn't get out if I wanted to. Which I do, desperately." I began to cry, softly.

"Fuck!" Simon said loudly. "Can you see anything you can identify out of the window. This is very important, Suzie. I have a bad feeling about this."

"It's dark now Simon, and we seem to be out in the countryside now. Just fields and lights off into the distance," I sobbed.

"Try and keep calm then. He will have to stop sometime. Tell him you need the toilet urgently. Maybe he will stop then."

I banged on the window. "Hey. You! I need the toilet now, desperately. So, unless you want a puddle in your cab I suggest that you find one. Or, at the very least pull over so I can go at the side of the road." I shouted.

Nothing. The guy acted nonplussed, and didn't respond to my pleas.

Oh, fuck, what is happening to me. I thought.

"Simon, he is totally blanking me. No response, despite my knocking on the window. I am getting really scared now."

"We'll find you, baby girl. Sweetheart, try not to do anything to antagonise him, but, if you get the chance to catch someone's attention, or run, go for it. I am going to speak to Al now. Maybe we can track your phone. Did you see the name of the cab company?"

I was just about to look for something, anything that could tell me more when the car stopped. Abruptly.

I flew off the seat, my phone flying from my hand onto the floor, as the doors opened and I was grabbed roughly by the hair.

"There you are, sweetheart."

I gasped, as I recognised the voice. It was Charles.

Jesus, he has me. What will he do with no one to stop him? I am dead meat. I thought.

A cloth was placed over my nose, and mouth, then everything went black.

CHAPTER 14

I gradually came to, groggy, and with blurred vision, unable to understand, at first, what was happening, or where I was. Then, with crystal clarity it came to me. Charles had me, and I had no clue where I was, or what his intentions were. But I doubted that his intentions were honourable in the least.

I thought to myself: *The taxi driver must have been in on it. Kidnapped.* My heart racing, as I began to examine my prison. For, surely, that was what this was.

It was dark, dank, and had an all-pervading smell of mould. It had to be a cellar of some kind.

I was lying on a double bed. Its metal frame was rusted in places, with an iron bedstead at the top and bottom. I could feel metal encasing my wrist, and realised that I was wearing a manacle. A chain snaked across the bed and was attached to a large metal ring set into the wall.

I pulled on it a few times, but to no avail. This was no flimsy chain, but a thick stainless-steel affair.

A thin cotton sheet, with a threadbare blanket, was my only bedding, offering very little protection against the all-pervading coldness.

I knew immediately, that under the covers, I was naked. My nipples were abraded by the rough thread of the sheets, goose bumps covered my skin, and the hairs on my body were standing to attention. Shivering uncontrollably, I continued to inspect the room.

Oh, my God, it was a dungeon. A single bulb lit the area, throwing ominous shadows around the room. It was large and, in places, water ran down the walls, forming puddles on the floor.

Ominous dark patches stood out, in contrast against the pale concrete floor.

A St Andrews cross sat smack in the middle of the room, and mirrors lined the wall opposite the bed. Their reflection marred, where the silver had worn away, giving a distorted view of the room.

Along the left-hand wall was a large device. A rack. I shuddered at the sight of it. It was something I would expect to find in a medieval torture chamber.

It was akin to a raised wooden bed, but there, the similarities to a bed ended. It had chains and restraints made from thick leather. I could make out the various pulleys and levers that could be used to stretch, and even possibly dislocate bones, or worse.

The opposite side of the bed held a cage, the kind often used in pet play. Although no evidence of kitty, or puppy toys were evident.

Looking back towards the St Andrews cross I spotted a suspension rig, sometimes referred to as a sex sling. I had a feeling that pleasure was the last thing that I could expect in this room.

Last, but not least was the endless rows of any number of toys that hung behind the rack. I spotted whips, floggers, tawse, canes, ball gags, and chains. In fact, an almost endless array of toys that could, or should I say would, be used for a combination of pain and pleasure. Once again, I doubted that giving me pleasure was his goal, as it would be far from Charles's sadistic mind.

Although still feeling a bit fuzzy, I turned, lowering my feet to the icy floor. The urge to pee was overwhelming.

Although a little unsteady I managed to stand, with the blanket wrapped around me as best I could, and spotted a metal chamber pot under the bed.

With no other options visible, or toilet facilities in sight, I pulled it out, thankful that, at least, it appeared clean.

I looked around once more, and listened for a few moments. I had absolutely no desire to be caught in the act, and quickly relieved myself. I placed the pot back under the bed, as the last thing I needed was for it to tip over.

That was when, on closer inspection I spotted a tap and drain between the bed and the rack.

I grabbed the pot, emptying it into the drain, and gave it a rinse clean, the nurse in me, taking over.

I pulled the thin sheet off the bed and wrapped that around myself, over the blanket. I gingerly walked in each direction as far as I could, until the chain became taut.

The door appeared to be a stout wooden door with a metal grill, a wooden shutter on the other side. As you would expect to find in an old prison.

Nothing obvious was visible that might aid me in getting free.

The biting cold seeped into my chilled toes, spreading quickly through my feet, and my teeth began to chatter incessantly. Any residual heat I had in my body, long gone.

Perhaps I won't die at Charles's hands. Maybe hypothermia will get to me first, I pondered, as the frigid air continued to gnaw at my flesh.

I retreated to the bed, curling my feet under me, trying to warm my cold, numb feet with whatever meagre warmth I had left in my core.

I had no sense of the passage of time, as there were no windows in this part of the cellar. So, after an indeterminate time I jumped, as I heard a key turning and a latch being lifted.

Scrambling back on the bed, as far back as possible. I waited, with bated breath. My heart was pounding violently in my chest. My breath now ragged, sweat beading my brow, despite the biting cold of the cellar.

The door creaked open and there he stood, watching me from the entrance. Unmoving. The smug smile on his face belied his innate ability to inflict pain and degradation, and the utter pleasure he derived from doing so.

Charles was fond of mind games, so I waited, nervously anticipating his next move. He knew this would raise my anxiety: mind fucks after all, had always been one of his specialities. Even knowing this didn't aid me, as I fought to breathe evenly, in and out. I was shaking violently as my fists clutched at the blanket, bunching it up. My knuckles whitened under the extreme pressure. Tears pooled as my stomach knotted. I felt sick with worry as bile rose in my throat.

"Good evening, Sweetness." He began quietly. "I see you discovered the chamber pot that I left you. Good Girl. An especially Good Girl that you worked out how to empty and clean it, too."

I cringed and jerked my head up, my eyes darting from one corner of the room to the other. Now I could pinpoint the tiny cameras dotted around the room, so small, that I must have missed them earlier with my blurry vision.

Fuck! I didn't see them before.

I curled up into the foetal position, cringing. But it was to no avail. I had no escape. No one knew where I was. No white knight was going to come to my rescue, this time.

Squeezing my eyes tightly shut, I waited. I detected his steps, coming closer as they echoed in the silent cellar.

I could sense him, towering over me where I lay.

"Now then, my sweet," he said softly, leaning closer. "First things first. Let's get you all cleaned up, shall we?"

I thought about the cold water tap at the back of the bed, and shuddered at the thoughts of becoming any colder than I already was.

To my astonishment, he produced a key, undid the manacle and then picked me up. Carrying me towards the door.

Where was he taking me now? I wondered.

He carried me through the doorway, and down a short corridor. Other doors like the one into the dungeon, were visible on either side, two to the left and two to the right. Ahead of us was a flight of steep stairs which he carried me carefully and gently up.

He produced yet another key at the top of the stairs, and unlocked the door. This led into a beautiful, bespoke kitchen with dark wooden units, a range cooker and Aga. Spic and span, and remarkably empty, it looked like no one had ever used this kitchen very much.

I glimpsed, through the window, a beautiful, but wild garden. It stretched into the distance.

We entered a large, open hallway, with classic black and white tiles. The hallway was huge, giving me some measure of the size of the house.

I was being kept captive in what appeared to be a mansion. This was not the same house we had met up in previously. The house he had taken me to before was a regular, family-sized, three bedroomed residence in the suburbs.

"Do you like this, my sweet? I inherited it when my Uncle died, many years ago. It's very secluded. No neighbours for miles around. As I am financially secure I thought keeping this would be a good investment."

He was sending me a message with this snippet of information. He believed there would be no rescue for me. No one would find me here. *Shit. I can't give up yet. Not yet. I need to cling on to the hope that someone will find me, and soon.*

"I have brought many of my especial treasures here, for entertainment over the years. As you saw, the place is adapted accordingly. To cater for my inclinations. If you behave, and do as you are told, sweetness, you will get to remain upstairs in warmth and luxury. Only visiting the dungeons when we play. But, if you are disobedient, and a brat, I am afraid I will have no option but to punish you. Do you understand, Sweetness?"

I tried to talk, but only managed a small croak. I was still trembling, even though the upstairs portions of the house were heated.

"I didn't hear you, Sweetness. You will have to make a better impression on me than that. Do. You. Understand?"

I managed to whisper, "Yes, Sir."

"Better. Let's try that one more time, though."

"Yes, Sir." I managed to speak a little louder. I knew better than to disobey.

I was his captive. Better to play his games, for now, until I could figure out an escape plan.

He continued to carry me, up a broad, sweeping staircase, and along a landing, then into the first bedroom. It was impressive, and I assumed it must be the Master bedroom. Plush navy furnishings were offset by cream accessories. We walked past an immense four-poster bed.

I'd seen a similar bed at an exhibition I had attended, a year or so ago. It was an expensive bondage bed, with a cage underneath, and fixing points on each of the solid oak bedposts. The bedhead had cuffs attached on chains and the bottom of the bed bore a strong resemblance to the pillories of medieval times. Holes were inset, for a head and wrists to be secured.

Before I could scrutinise anything else in detail, he started moving again, toward a door to the left. A well-proportioned *en-suite* bathroom lay beyond.

This, again, had obviously been adapted, with ties set into the tiled walls, and suspension points in the ceiling. A Victorian claw foot bath dominated the room, and picture windows with views yet again of the surrounding countryside beyond. There were lights in the distance.

He walked past the bath, and set me on my feet next to a large, walk-in shower. Taking a pair of steel handcuffs from a side table, he had me secure again in moments.

"Do. Not. Move. Understand?" He said.

"Yes, Sir." I replied.

He watched me for a few moments, then reached over and began to fiddle with the dials. Water began to cascade down from the huge rainfall showerhead overhead and jetting out from the various smaller jets set into the walls. Satisfied that the water was the right temperature, he pulled me toward him, pulling at and discarding my sheet and blanket, in a flash.

"Present, Sweetness." He commanded, and I put my feet further apart, and stood up tall with my eyes lowered. I would give him no excuse to punish me. I could do this. I had to survive this ordeal, and gain his trust in order to break free.

My jaw rigid, teeth clenched, I stood awaiting my fate.

"So, beautiful, Sweetness," Charles cooed, quickly disrobing himself. I heard the zipper descend on his pants as I lifted my eyes slightly. His cock was rigid, bolt upright, pre-cum oozing from the engorged purple tip, indicating his arousal.

Setting his Saville Row suit, and white button-down shirt neatly on a chair close by, he pushed his shoes underneath his socks discarded on top of the pile of clothes.

"Come here, Sweetness," he ordered and I stepped forward as he guided me into the shower. Undoing the cuffs briefly, he then refastened them to a tie suspended on a metal pipe, next to the showerhead.

My arms stretched high above me. He manoeuvred my feet wider and, from a shelf close by, produced a large metal spreader bar, which he promptly attached to each ankle.

He stepped back slightly, to admire his handiwork from each angle. Satisfied that I was adequately secured and unable to fight back, he began to bathe me.

Gently. Lovingly almost.

This contrast in behaviour was confusing and disturbing.

Using a flannel, he carefully but firmly cleansed my body. Every. Single. Inch.

Despite my trepidation and his gentleness, this was unsettling, as each time he moved to a fresh spot the urge to cringe away, was overwhelming.

Just as I was wondering when the other shoe would drop, he struck.

Quite literally.

Catching me unawares, he slapped my right breast, with such force that I saw a starburst behind my eyelids as I squeezed them tight shut in response.

As he struck my left breast I bit down on my lower lip, my limbs trembling.

I hissed in pain then moaned out loud and flinched as I saw him raise his hand.

The taste of copper in my mouth revealed that I had bitten through my lower lip at the second strike.

The third strike never happened.

Panting, my nostrils flaring, I stood clenching my teeth, awaiting his next move.

Light-headed, and a little dizzy, I tried to remain perfectly, still so as not to raise his ire further.

"A little taste of the punishments you will receive for your disobedience, my Sweet One," he growled. "You are, and always will be, my property, my pet. The sooner you understand this fact, the better your treatment will be."

He reached up and undid the cuffs, and then the spreader bar. I sagged in relief, my arms tingling and a little numb after being raised so long.

He proceeded to snag a large white towelling robe from a hook nearby, and helped me into it.

My heart rate had levelled out a little but I was still a bit befuddled and clumsy. Shaking and shivering, but not from cold this time. The aftermath of my fight or flight response.

Who knew what his next move would be? I thought.

He pulled me close, and began to pat my hair dry with a fresh towel, having wrapped another around his own waist. Then he led me mechanically out of the bathroom. As I tried to concentrate on just putting one foot, in front of the other. In a daze.

He led me across the room, and I found myself standing with my back to the bed.

"Sit, Sweetness," He ordered. I obeyed, my mind working overtime, as I tried to rationalise my situation.

CHAPTER 15

I could see dawn approaching, as the sun rose in the distance. It must have been the start of a new day. I had been unconscious longer than I thought. I never expected to wake up still in his bed.

I needed to buy myself some time. I should play along with his nasty games and earn his trust.

My stomach growled, loudly.

"Hungry, Sweetness?" he sneered.

"Yes, Sir." I replied.

"I think you need to earn breakfast, sweetness. Don't you? Now then, I need to think of something special for your next punishment." He appeared to be talking to himself at this point.

He stood, towering over me, for what felt like the longest of times. He was clearly debating what punishment, I would receive.

He knew all my hard limits, so I expected him to do something particularly nasty from that list.

His face softened a little, and the ghost of a smile appeared.

He sat alongside me on the bed and I automatically cringed away, but he was having none of that.

"If I remember rightly, you were always partial to a bit of OTK spanking. I presume that hasn't changed. So, observe the position now, Sweetness." And he proceeded to pat his knee.

This puzzled me, as spanking is high up as one of my favourites on my list of fetishes.

"Now! "He boomed, and I moved into position as quick as I could. Yet I could hear him tutting.

"Now, my pet, I think you know better than to present across my knee wearing a robe. Don't you, my Sweet?"

I stood quickly and discarded the robe across the bottom of the bed and regained my position over his lap. My arse cheeks were available for him to punish, at his will.

He began by rubbing. Gently at first, then he began to slap alternating cheeks lightly. Basically, he was warming me up.

This threw me, as I was expecting to be soundly thrashed from the get go.

The slaps began to land harder, and faster. Then his fingers were thrust into my pussy and he snarled, "See, my Pet. So, fucking wet for me. Soaking. I knew I could get your juices flowing. Why would you think you could escape me so easily?" My body had betrayed me. Then, he shouted louder. "You. Are. Mine. Slut."

Each word punctuated with a resounding slap. I clenched my buttocks, my ears ringing and tears flowing freely down my face.

Then, he changed his timing so that I wasn't sure when the next blow would fall.

Then. He stopped. Dead.

Whereas when we had played initially I would receive a little aftercare at this point, none was forthcoming.

He pushed me off his knee and I fell heavily to the floor. Immediately curling up into the foetal position, I then lay perfectly still. I was shaking badly from the sudden change of circumstances.

"Up, slut." He commanded, and I rose unsteadily and went straight into the present position, visibly trembling.

He rose over me, and pointed to the end of the bed.

"Position yourself with your hands on the foot of the bed, and grip the bedrail. Bend over, ready for your next punishment."

"Yes, Sir," I mumbled.

"Speak up, slut." He said.

"Yes, Sir!" I replied, louder this time.

I clutched the rail so hard that my knuckles were white. My flaming bottom was extended, legs apart, in readiness for my next ordeal. *Was my torment never to end? Charles was harsh as a Dom, but never like this. Never this brutal. I don't want to antagonise him in any way.*

I heard him cross the room, and the creak of a door, but whether it was the wardrobe door, or the door to the room, I had no way of knowing.

Once more footfalls moved behind me, and I awaited my fate.

With the first strike, I knew immediately which implement he was using. A tawse.

It had been one of my favourite toys when we used to play. But, I had a feeling that this would change after today. Charles was playing with my mind, and a total mind-fuck seemed to be his goal. I needed to stay strong, or he would win, and I needed to believe that my Doms would find me, and rescue me.

The noise of the hit sounded like a bullwhip, cracking through the air. The hit blossomed immediately into an intense fiery pain.

Then, I couldn't stop myself from reacting, as I moved forward and to the side slightly, in an attempt to avoid the next blow.

The second stroke landed in a slightly different spot. Once again, I flinched and moved, letting out a grunt as I did. My buttocks were on fire, as he proceeded to pepper both cheeks with a previous unfelt fervour.

Then, he hit my sweet spot, just where the buttock and my upper leg met.

Sobbing, tears pouring down my cheeks and snot running down. I bit my lip so hard I could taste the coppery flavour of my own blood again.

As he hit time and time again with no let up.

Just as I was about to collapse in pain, he stopped. As I stood there, the overwhelming throbbing pain carried on growing. Intense burning shot through me as I fought to stay upright, fighting against the need to sink to the floor.

"Hmmm… that will do for starters, my Sweet. I think maybe you just earned yourself a bit of food, and a sip of water," he sneered.

I tried to stand, and each tiny movement brought fresh waves of pain. Shaking I reached behind me to run my hand over the source of my pain, and felt wetness. He had broken the skin so badly that rivulets of blood were seeping out, and dripping down the back of my thighs.

He hit my hands away with a swift slap.

"Did I say you could touch, slut?" He growled. "I asked a question, Pet?"

I instantly replied, nervously, "No. Sir," as I observed the present position, unable to even imagine what else he had in store for me.

"Good Girl," he said.

I thought to myself, *if this is for starters, what more can I expect? How the hell am I going to survive this?*

But I knew I had to try. The longer I held out, the more time Simon and Alistair would have to find me. I didn't doubt that they would look for me.

Charles produced a collar, and a leash. Reaching over, he secured the collar around my throat, then tightened it, leaving me very little room, even to swallow.

He jerked the leash once, and I scurried behind him, clumsily, endorphins giving me mixed messages.

It was then that I finally saw his naked back. I had seen the front of him naked previously, but never a back view. He must have put on his pants, socks and shoes when I was waiting at the bed. But for some reason, no shirt this time.

Somehow, he had managed to evade my seeing his back. Now, I knew why. The crazy criss-cross pattern of scars that marred the surface were not accidental. Someone had spent a lot of energy marking his back in such a manner. They were old scars too. Silvery, and broad. Keloid scars.

Those are left when someone has been tortured and no medical treatment been given. There didn't seem to be an inch that wasn't covered in them. They ran from his shoulders, and down into the bottom of his back.

What the fuck? Is this why he is such a fucking pig? Jesus, who would do such a thing? Why would you do something like that to another human being?

We took the reverse journey from earlier, and soon I was actually glad to be able to stop and catch my breath, as he proceeded to manacle me to the tie on the wall.

He removed the leash, but not the collar. Out of his pants pocket he produced a small silver metal padlock, and ordered.

"Kneel, slut, with your back towards me." I obeyed quickly. "Lift your hair, Sweet." he sneered.

I knew exactly what the significance of the padlock was. He was further marking me as his, by padlocking the collar in place. He tightened the collar a little more, not so much that I couldn't breathe or that it choked me, but so that I couldn't get my fingers underneath. With the padlock in position, he took the key and placed it once again in his pocket saying," I will keep this safe, my Pet."

I stayed stock still, as I hadn't been given permission to move and didn't want to risk further punishments unnecessarily.

"Good Girl," he said, almost sounding sincere. "I will be back with some food and drink in a short while."

As if on command, my stomach growled, loudly. My mouth was parched. I heard him leave, and the key click as he locked the door. A short while later I heard the door creak open again, and footsteps approach.

"Turn around, slut, and observe the standing present position."

I caught a glimpse of what I was being served. A meagre bowl of thin porridge, a paper cup full of water and some toast on a paper plate. More than I expected, to be honest.

He placed the bowl, cup and plate on the floor, and wished me a quick "Enjoy". Then he turned, and left abruptly, slamming the door for good measure on the way out.

I stood there for a while, worried that he would return, and try and find a further excuse to punish me.

There were no utensils, but, as luck would have it, the porridge was thin enough to drink. I made short shrift of my rations and sat down, sipping my water. I could see no point in saving it, as there was an abundant supply via the tap on the wall.

Once I finished eating and drinking I lay face down on the bed. My hot arse cheeks throbbed in time with my heart beat. I rubbed at them gingerly, in an attempt to soothe them, hardly registering the cold due to the heat of the flesh. Yet, after a while, I once again had to wrap the thin covers around my bruised, and battered body. The cellar was cold and damp, especially in comparison to the warm rooms upstairs, in the main parts of the house.

Before long, despite the pain radiating from my bottom, I fell into an unsettled sleep.

I awoke sometime later, still exhausted despite having slept, and tried to determine if there was any hope of escape.

As I attempted to sit up, the pain hit me full force and I groaned. It had faded a little from the time before I fell asleep, but it was still omnipresent. A reminder of my place, and a portent of what was to come. I was sure I could expect more of the same, or possibly worse.

I began to examine my surroundings afresh, but eventually began to succumb to overwhelming despair. I couldn't see any avenue of escape. Was this how I would end my days? Turned from a willing submissive into an enslaved captive?

Surely someone will have noticed my disappearance, but how would they know where I am?

I lost track of time. Was it night-time now? Or, possibly, the next day? My stomach began growling, as hunger began to claw at me. Would Charles allow me to slowly starve to death? Who knew what he was capable of?

As if on cue, I heard approaching footsteps, then the click of the key in the lock.

I was torn between remaining under the covers, in what little warmth they offered, or fighting back in the only way I could.

If I could just get a little more freedom. Perhaps I should pretend to accept my fate, by being a good little submissive. Maybe, then, I stood a chance of escaping.

CHAPTER 16

Decision made, I got up swiftly, groaning as I did and took the present position. Trying desperately hard to keep still, despite the cold. Goosebumps rose over my body and all the hairs stood to attention. Not in arousal, but because the cold was striking through me quickly as my feet hit the cold concrete floor. I kept my eyes lowered.

I heard his approach, and resisted to urge to raise my eyes. I had to be strong.

"Well. Well. Well, my Sweet. I knew you still felt something for me, and that you were still mine."

He reached forward and squeezed my nipples, hard as he could, digging his fingernails in as he did.

I couldn't help but close my eyes in response, and gasp. *Fuck* I thought. *Shit, that hurts*. But I held my position as he finally let go.

I heard a rattle, then opened my eyes, spotting the clover clamps, connected by a chain, in his hands.

Shit. I hate clover clamps. I thought. *Christ on a bike, my nipples are sensitive enough as it is. Those things are nasty little fuckers. Brutal*.

First, he nipped my right nipple, attaching the first of the clamps. I hissed in response. Then, my left nipple was tweaked. Clover clamps can be harsh, especially in the wrong hands. Especially in HIS hands.

Pain radiated through my body, as he lifted the chain and yanked, commanding, "Open, slut."

I knew instantly what he wanted me to open. My mouth. Charles had done this before when we played, but then he had used pleasure to offset the pain.

No pleasure was forthcoming this time, though, as he placed the chain in my mouth.

"Close, Slut." He ordered.

I obeyed instantly, and the chain pulled hard at my tender nipples, as my eyes welled with tears.

"Good Girl," he said as he began to move away. "Keep still, and I will return shortly. You do NOT want to disobey me, Slut. The consequences will be dire, if you do."

With cameras watching my every move, I had little choice. God knows what punishment would ensue, if I disobeyed.

Timed passed painfully slowly, as I stood there. Cold, in pain, and feeling utterly lost. I clamped my jaw closed around the chain.

This time, I wasn't even aware of his approach, but heard the distant creak of the cellar door opening.

The pain from my breasts was excruciating, and my jaw ached from the pressure of keeping the chain in my mouth.

Tears ran down my face as I squeezed my eyes tight shut. I was frightened that if I opened my eyes I would let go of the chain, risking further torture. Trembling, but not in need, due to terror.

I could sense Charles stood in front of me, and then he spoke.

"This is the potential I saw in you. This is why you will be the mine forever. I'm so happy you finally saw the light, and decided to obey me." He reached up and took the chain from my mouth and I breathed a sigh of relief, which was short-lived as the throbbing from my breasts did not abate. Each movement of the chain sent a jolt of pain through my entire body.

Charles then released first one, then the other nipple from the bite of the clamps. I gasped and whimpered, as the blood began to flow through them. It was akin to hot needles being pushed through each one. He moved closer, and suckled each nipple avidly, reducing the sting only slightly. I tried hard not to react, and cringe away. A knot was developing in my stomach, due to the tension I felt at this act.

"Come." He pulled me to the bed, and began to unlock the manacle from around my wrist. "I hope you have an appetite, as I have some food prepared. "

With that comment, he led me from the cellar and back up into the kitchen. Unbelievably, it was evening again. I must have slept longer than I thought. No wonder my stomach was growling, and felt so empty.

We carried on through, into a room I hadn't seen before, a sumptuous dining room. Heavy burgundy velvet drapes framed the large French windows, showing the darkened gardens beyond. The décor was akin to something from a regency romance novel. A mahogany table centre stage, and eight matching chairs. A huge ornate sideboard held decanters of some amber liquid, I presumed to be brandy, or whisky.

A sparkling chandelier twinkled above, and the table was already set for two. Puzzling!

Crystal glasses, gilt edged crockery. *This is like some bizarre scene from Beauty and the Beast. I have absolutely no clue what is going to happen next. Was this some sort of game? Or did he truly think he could change me so easily? That I would submit to him so soon?*

Despite the warmth of the room, I shivered constantly. Feeling vulnerable in my nakedness, and exposed. This was too easy. There had to be a catch. I had to keep my guard up, and keep him sweet.

"Sit, my Sweet," he said, and pointed to the chair on the left-hand side of the table, which faced towards the windows. He pulled the chair out slightly, and I sat down, stiffly. My sore bottom reminded me of yesterday's gruelling punishments. My body was a battleground of hurt. I noticed, then, that there were serving dishes with lids on the table. Condensation on the metal surfaces indicated that something hot was inside.

I watched him furtively as he walked behind me and picked up a carafe of red wine, which he then proceeded to pour into my glass. After which he took the seat next to me, and picked up a little silver bell. He rang it twice, and we were no longer alone.

A young girl, dressed in a sexy parody of a maid's outfit, entered. She began to remove the lids from the food, and serve us silently. She looked very young, barely out of her teens. She was very pretty, with bright, sea green eyes, and silky long blonde hair to her waist. She retrieved the carafe, and poured some wine for Charles, returning it to its original position on the sideboard.

Holy fuck. I thought. *How many of us are there here? This is beyond bizarre.*

She placed vegetables, meat and gravy onto the plates in front of us, then stood to one side observing the present position, eyes lowered.

"Thank you, Sweetness." He said, "Leave us now."

With that, she was gone. She hadn't uttered a single word, or acknowledged me in any way. *Was she here willingly? Or, was she like me? A prisoner?*

"Tuck in, my Pet. "he commanded. "You look like you have lost some weight already, over the last three days."

I couldn't help my reaction as I gasped. *I had been here three days? I thought it would be two tops.* My tension increased and my heart began to race. My mouth was watering as I felt the bile rise in my throat. My breathing increased and I had to concentrate hard to slow it down again, as I picked up my knife and fork.

I took a couple of deep breaths to steady myself, and pushed a fork into a carrot. It took all my willpower to then put it to my lips, and begin to chew. I told myself: *Be strong. Help must be on its way by now. It must be, or I am lost. I need to eat to survive and to keep warm in that awful cellar.*

I could feel Charles' eyes on me, watching my every move. He was a Dom, after all, and used to looking for subtle signs. Any indication that I was not falling in with his plans, any nuance of body language, that told him of the abhorrence I felt for him, and I would know about it.

His previous punishments would be nothing compared to what he would do with me, if he knew of my thoughts. Of my need to escape.

I continued to eat for a few minutes, before he seemed to relax, and began to eat also. Picking up my wine, I took a long swig. *Dutch courage,* I thought. We didn't speak, just sat eating and drinking, as if this was the most normal thing to do in the world. Me, sat naked and bruised, as we ate dinner.

"More wine, my Sweet?" He asked, and I nodded. Unsure if I was even allowed to talk. Not risking it. "Lost your voice, my Sweet?" he said.

"No, Sir. Sorry, Sir" I replied quietly.

I continued to eat, but the food seemed tasteless, as I chewed mechanically. Swallowing down past the lump in my throat. I managed to eat all that was on my plate and began to sip at the second glass of wine Charles had poured for me. I noticed that he only drank one himself, as his hard-glittering eyes watched me closely.

"I think we are done here, my sweet." Charles said. "Time to get back to your training, I believe. "

He stood slowly, and stepped to the back of my chair as I stood.

I began to swallow constantly, and would have played with my hair, a thing I do when I am nervous, or agitated. But I knew that my body language would give me away. We weren't together long, but long enough for him to know my tells.

Unbelievably, he allowed me some bathroom time to myself. I didn't dare check out the bathroom as he would realise what I was doing. I needed to play my part well, for him to be convinced of my complete submission.

I exited the downstairs bathroom, and observed the present position in front of him, as he sat in the winged-back chair in the corner. He dropped his head to one side, observing me critically. His legs crossed, casually. A tilt of his lips showed his amusement at my response.

"Good Girl," he drawled as he tilted his head the other way. Somewhat similar to the way a dog moves his head from side to side, as they listen.

I was powerless, and he knew that. All I could do was wait, and see what unfolded. *What games and toys would he subject my body to, next?*

I was unsure what would be preferable, punishment and pain, or, if he wanted me to pleasure him. Or even, God forbid, to have sex with him. I shuddered at the thought.

"Cold? My pet? "He asked.

"A little, Sir." I replied.

"Well, maybe we need to do something to warm you up, then?" He snickered.

I managed to put a fake smile on my face, as he stretched out his hand to take mine and pull me from the floor. I took his hand tentatively, and wondered how long I would have to maintain this charade?

Once again, I was led up to the Master Suite upstairs. He indicated that I go in front of him, as we ascended the stairs to his room. I could feel the heat radiating from his body as we did.

No shower this time, but I was led into the room and ordered to kneel at the foot of the bed. My eyes lowered, I waited in trepidation. What fresh tortures would today bring?

I could hear him banging about in the cupboard, or maybe the wardrobe. I knew better than to lift my head to find out which one. The only result would be a harsher punishment.

"Eyes up, Slut." He commanded. "Time for you to give me some pleasure, I believe. Attend to my needs, instead of yours, before we continue."

He thought that what he did to me, gave me pleasure? If that was pleasure, what further torments could I expect? Then, I thought about the rack in the dungeon, and the medieval torture devices I saw earlier, and the cage. *Which would it be, should he even suspect my motives?*

He moved closer, and I could see the hard length of him, outlined against his pants. He began to unbuckle his belt, and the sound of his zipper slowly descending made me shudder. The bile was already rising in my throat, as I thought about what he was now expecting me to perform.

Lord, give me strength. I feel sick at the mere thought of it. Charles wasn't small either, in length, or in girth. *There's a good chance the first time he rams his cock in my throat, I will throw up. This is not going to be good. I need to do this without putting what I have just eaten, all over his expensive shoes. Or I can guarantee, the shit will hit the fan.*

He moved closer still, and demanded. "Open up, My Sweet. I suggest, if you want to keep those lovely pearly white teeth that you make sure I don't have a chunk taken out of me. No. Teeth." He emphasised.

OMG. He actually believes that I have submitted to him. That I am doing this now, because I want to, and I get turned on by it! Oh God, I hope I can get through this without being sick. Even the mere thought of his cock in my mouth is making my stomach roll.

I took a deep breath, and opened my mouth wide, closing my eyes, so I didn't have to look at him. *Maybe, I can pretend it is Simon, or Alistair?*

"Now, now, my Sweet. I want to watch your beautiful face, as you take me deep in your throat. I want to see those eyes water, as I fuck your throat hard, and watch you swallow down all I have to give you" he purred.

He thrust his hips forcefully forward, hitting the back of my throat as he pushed hard, fucking my throat brutally.

From Willing Sub To Enslaved Captive

Water began to pool, and overflow from my mouth. I began to gag almost immediately, as he grabbed a fistful of my hair, dragging my head back to enable him to force his cock in further.

I was desperately trying not to gag. But, controlling my gag reflex wasn't easy at the best of times. Especially when it was someone that basically, made my skin crawl. It was nigh on impossible.

The drool was now thick and stringy and beginning to slip from the corner of my mouth, and onto my chest. My stomach rolled again, as I tasted his pre-cum. Salty in my mouth.

With deliberate, hard stokes, tempo increasing, his cock hit the back of my throat. Aggressively, with force, again, and again with no respite.

He pulled out, and smiled as the long string of saliva stretched down from his cock head and dripped down my side.

He plunged back in, hard and fast. Pace increasing, as I felt him grow in my mouth rapidly. Choking and gagging, I felt his cum spray into the back of my throat. My eyes watered as tears ran freely down my face. He smiled, he was loving this, the power of the act.

"Swallow, Bitch," he commanded, and despite my queasy stomach, I obeyed. I had no choice but to obey. I swallowed, and struggle to swallowed again. Unable to breathe, trying to breathe through my nose as my mouth was assailed with gallons of warm, thick, salty cum. Panicking as I was overwhelmed with the sheer quantity of cum I had to deal with.

I needed to make him think I was enjoying this. That I loved the taste of his cum. As I struggled to breathe, and hold in the contents of my stomach. He was holding my head tight, thrusting still, as he milked his cock with my throat.

I repeated the mantra in my head. *Relax your throat. Try not to tense. Try not to gag* as I struggled with my inability to draw a proper breath, trying to breath around his monstrous cock, that had impaled my throat. My lungs were desperate in my panic to breathe, and not be sick. His fists tightened in my hair, as he let out a loud groan.

Finally, his cock began to soften. *Thank fuck for that,* I thought, as I continued to consciously control my visceral reactions to his actions.

"Now then, Slut. Do a proper job of it, and clean me up," he demanded.

I waited a moment, and then tried and to do as he commanded, sticking my tongue out trepidatiously, and then it hit me. There was no controlling my reaction to this. My mouth filled with saliva instinctively, as I felt my stomach contracting violently. This final command was a step too far. My stomach muscles clenched, over and over, as the contents of my stomach were expelled, propelled from my body, spraying over both his lower half, and pooling on the floor over his once shiny, black shoes.

CHAPTER 17

"**W**hat the fuck?" He screams out at me. "Shit. You bitch. What the fuck is that all about? What slut doesn't know how to give a decent blow job, without hurling?" He moved quickly backwards, almost tripping in his haste, as his pants fall around his ankles.

Shit. Despite the circumstances, and the fact that my stomach was still determined to empty every morsel from it. I almost laughed out loud. *Christ almighty. Control yourself, Suzie. The shit is already going to hit the fan big style. The last thing I need is to make matters worse.*

The smell was horrible. Vile. I was almost sick again and started to gag. The congealed undigested food, still warm and slimy, was all over my knees, and had pooled around me.

Charles had disappeared into the bathroom. I wouldn't have been shocked if he wasn't being sick himself. I know I would have been, if someone had hurled all over me. I heard the shower and then sat there trying to calm my stomach. Willing myself to stay in place, so as not to make the situation any worse than it was. If that was even possible.

I heard the water stop, and then he was striding towards me. A stern look on his face.

I couldn't move. I stayed absolutely still and lowered my eyes in terror. Tears were dripping down my face, as I waited for the inevitable.

It seemed like an age had passed, but it could only have been minutes, when I heard him say. "Girl, look up. I think you need a clean-up, don't you? Now stand." His stern face was making me nervous.

I stood, uncertainly, not sure what a **clean-up** would entail. I didn't get a chance to think about it, as he grabbed me roughly by the arm and dragged me towards the bathroom.

"Get in the bath, slut," he commanded, and when I didn't move quickly enough for him, he picked me up and plonked me in the empty bath.

How the hell can I have a bath with no water in it? I thought. Then I got to find out exactly how that could happen, as a blast of cold water hit me across the chest and I fall backwards into the tub.

Fuck, Shit. What the fucking hell? Arrgh, I thought. *For fucks sake, that is icy cold.*

Charles continued to blast me with freezing cold water. Every inch of me was now sopping wet, including my hair. Satisfied finally, that he had removed any trace of contamination from my body he turned off the jet of water.

I lay there, shivering. So, cold, that my teeth were chattering uncontrollably and my nipples extended, painfully.

Shit! I thought when I got hypothermia, it would be when I was in the dungeon. Not the upstairs of the house.

Charles had wandered off for a few minutes. So, I sat still, wondering what my next move should be. When he returned, unexpectedly, he was carrying a large bath towel, and a big fluffy dressing gown.

I still didn't move, uncertain as to what was happening now.

"Well, stand up. So that I can dry you. You must be freezing cold sat there, Sweetheart," he said.

- 127 -

Stunned, I looked around the bathroom, confused. *Was he talking to me? What the heck is going on? Why the sudden change of heart? This is screwing with my head now.*

He continued to stand there, but had opened the huge bath towel for me to step into. I stood, with difficulty: I was so very cold, and shaking violently as I tried to step out onto the bathmat.

Charles grasped my hand, and helped me out. Then, he began to quickly pat me dry, rubbing my body, warming me. Once he had dried me, he opened the dressing gown and I pushed my arms through as he fastened the belt around me, snugly. Then he picked me up, and carried me into the bedroom. The covers had already been pulled back, and he laid me down on the side nearest the door. He pulled the covers up, then walked to the other side of the bed and began to undress.

I watched in fascination. His behaviour was so strange, I was unable to decide what his next move would be.

He watched me intently, as he proceeded to climb into the bed, and under the covers. I was unable to take my eyes off him, unsure what was happening. He reached over, and pulled me close. I was still icy cold, with my feet like two blocks of ice. Unperturbed, he pulled me closer still and wrapped his body around me. I held myself stiffly as long as I could, unable to compute such odd, contrary behaviour. That was until his warmth began to spread through my limbs. Lack of food, and the stress of the last few days, had taken its toll, and eventually I fell asleep.

My sleep was disturbed by horrific dreams where Charles alternately tortured, and drowned me. The worrying thing was, that that might not be far from the truth.

I awoke, still wrapped in Charles' arms. I lay as still as I could, so as not to disturb him. My head was banging, probably from dehydration. What little bit I ate and drank before I threw up, was inconsequential. My mouth was like sandpaper, and as I hadn't cleaned my teeth before I fell asleep it was almost as if I had fur coating my tongue. Very horrible flavoured fur. *I must smell like dog breath,* I thought.

Despite the lack of fluids, I really needed to pee. *What do I do? Just climb out of bed? I can't see that going down well. It is either that, or a very big puddle in the bed. Also, not a good way forward.* Luckily, or not as the case may be Charles chose that moment to awake.

"Good morning, my Pet. You were fidgeting so much you woke me up. I imagine you want to go to the toilet, so don't waste time and just do it. By the way, leave the door open this time. Time to up your training. Your body is mine, and I expect you to act accordingly. Nothing is to be kept secret from me."

What is it with Doms and their need to hear all their subs' bodily functions? I think it is plain gross. I grumbled in my head.

I finished off in the bathroom and returned to the bedroom. Not sure whether to get back into the bed, or to stand at the side, I dithered a little. Bad move. Very bad move.

Nice Charles was now absent, and nasty Charles had returned, in full force.

"For fuck's sake, Pet!" He shouted. "Just stand by the bed in present position. Your hovering around undecided is just plain irritating."

I assumed the position and stood there with bated breath. *Shit, I already knew about the dithering and his annoyance when I did it. Why did I forget that? What's wrong with me? Apart from hunger and thirst, that is!*

He climbed casually out of bed and walked around to check out my position, moving me a couple of times, making me place my feet wider than normal. Veritably growling as he did so. I kept my eyes lowered and hoped that the newfound version of Charles from last night was hanging around still. I definitely didn't want the horrible sadistic version administering more punishments. Even some dry bread and water would be very welcome, right now. Hunger pangs beset me constantly, and my stomach actually hurt, it was that empty.

He moved slowly, stretching out the time it took him to inspect me. Then demanded, "Stay right there, Slut, while I shower and get dressed. I expect even you will be able to manage that. Won't you?"

"Yes, Sir." I replied quickly.

He strode off into the bathroom and I could hear the shower running. I thought the shower was never going stop. It seems to carry on endlessly. He was doing this on purpose, making me wait. Finally, I heard footsteps as he came into the room, and waited patiently as he gathered up his fresh clothing and dressed.

After that, he approached again and inspected me once more, tutting as he did so.

He wants me to fail, I realised this but this reinforced that belief.

"Hmmm. Are you cold again, Sweetness? You are shaking like a leaf." He remarks. "Seems like I am always trying to warm you up. Doesn't it? Let's see if we can make a start on that and administer your punishment at the same time. Come."

The leash was once again fastened to my collar and he began to walk quickly toward the door. I should have known this was him just messing with my head again. I was so tired of his inconsistent behaviour. Hot then cold. Nasty then nice.

As we passed through the kitchen I noticed the snow falling again outside, and icicles hanging from the nearby bushes. Soon we were back to the cellar door, and as he opened the door the frigid air hit me instantly. I shuddered, in both fear, and with the cold.

He positioned me next to the bed and I stood still. I was scared to move a muscle, but I was shaking so much that it was difficult to stay in place. It was colder than before, as now I could see my breath in the iciness of the cellar. A fog appeared every time I breathed out. How long could I survive down here? As I looked down at my body, I could see for myself that I had lost weight. Not eating for virtually four days will do that to a body. How much more of this could I take? *God knows*.

I simply couldn't give up yet. Someone must be looking for me. I had people that loved me and would ask where I am. They would go to the police and report me missing. My mum and dad, Claire, and my newly found Sirs, too. Someone was going to be looking for me. I just needed to hang on, and find a way to become free. Do whatever it takes to gain my freedom.

I didn't raise my eyes, but, somehow, I managed to stand a little straighter. A little prouder.

Charles returned to stand in front of me and I tensed, waiting. That was what this was, now, a waiting game. A mind-fuck game too.

"Now then, I have decided what your next punishment will be. Come, my Pet." He indicated that I should follow, and picked up the leash as he leads me towards the medieval looking device. The rack.

"Climb up on the rack, my Sweet. I think you are going to enjoy this," he said.

I was shaking so badly that I found it difficult to climb up. My head was swimming as I tried repeatedly to pull myself up. I felt sick just looking at the pulleys and chains.

"I am losing my temper here a little, Sweetness," he said, raising his voice this time.

I tried again to climb up and managed to scramble up onto the rack. It's hard, unyielding surface was cold and damp. Charles indicated that I should shuffle up the rack, and set to fastening the straps and pulling at the chains until he was happy that I was secure.

My wrists were encased in leather straps, as were my ankles. These in turn were attached to chains, which led to the ropes that went around the large barrel at the head of the rack.

I watched out of the corner of my eye as he began to turn the wooden wheel, I felt the ropes go taut. At first, there was only a feeling of stretching. Nothing untoward, until he began to turn the wheel again. This time I started to feel a twinge in my joints. My wrists and ankles, then my spine began to ache. My breathing was ragged as I struggled to take in a breath. My skin, despite the extreme cold, became clammy. My heart was racing so fast that I could feel it hammering in my chest.

He couldn't possibly keep on doing this? Turning that wheel past this point? Could he?

Just as I thought this, I heard the wheel creak once more, and the ropes pulled, hard. I was beginning to panic now. I tensed, trying to pull back, to stop the progress of the ropes but that was to no avail. I thrashed my head from side to side. Simple physics was in play here, and I had no control over the pull. I grunted as I could feel the stretching once more. The pull on my wrists was growing stronger with each turn. My endorphins were kicking in a little. Although a masochist, I would hardly call myself a pain slut. But the next turn of the wheel has me groaning out loud, as I curse.

"Fuck."

The pain now seemed unrelenting. My joints and muscles were on fire. Although it began in my joints initially, it now radiated throughout my body. I felt on fire. I clenched my fists in response and shouted out again.

"Shit, Arrgh!"

I looked over at Charles, and saw the expression on his face. Bliss. He was loving inflicting this pain. My hair was now wet from sweat and beginning to stick to my head. I licked my lips nervously, as they began to crack at my constant licking.

I tried to distract myself, but that was when Charles started to talk to me.

"Sweetness," he said." Look at me, Sweetness. Now."

I obeyed as I had nothing left to fight with. My pain was growing and I really needed it to stop now.

"Good Girl," He said.

Fucking Good Girl. What the fuck is that all about.

"You have a safe word, my Sweet. Do you remember it? If you agree to wear my collar and sign a slave registration, and a non-disclosure agreement, maybe then, I could honour your safe word. What do you say, my Sweet?"

Tears had begun to course down the sides of my face and drip onto the wooden base of the rack. I opened my mouth to speak, but I had no clue what to say. What could I say?

Just as I thought about this, he gave the wheel a quick turn.

The pain was sharper this time, and I screamed out in agony, bowing off the wooden base which only increased the pain tenfold. Fear now enveloped me. I was scared shitless by this constant pain with no chance of relief. That was, unless I agreed. I would just have to say the word and this would end. I could live to fight another day. I could see him move towards the wheel again and screamed out.

"Yes. Yes. Yes, I agree. Whatever you want. I will sign anything. Just make this stop. Please make this stop." I sobbed as tears rolled down my face.

"Good Girl. Maybe just one more turn to be sure you mean it."

With that, he did a half a turn for effect. The pain was so excruciating that I felt physically sick. I felt faint and my vision blurred a little. I must have gone white or something as he quickly began to turn the wheel back then undid the cuffs on my wrists and ankles.

CHAPTER 18

I lay there, unable to move, initially. My body still sore and stiff. I was frightened to move until instructed to. After that demonstration of torture, I was unsure just how far he would go, and what he was capable of.

"Down you come, my sweet. I think maybe some porridge is in order now, and maybe a little sip of water. Don't want you collapsing on me, do I?" He joked.

He truly was deranged. Off his head. An utter nutter. I moved and stretched a little, trying to get the circulation back into my arms and legs, by rubbing at them. Finally, able to sit with care, I began to edge forwards. My knees were so wobbly that I wasn't sure if they would hold me up right now.

I slid over the edge and tentatively placed my feet on the floor. The cold seeped into them, instantly. *When would this end? Would I ever regain my freedom? And, what the fuck is he going to do with me next and why has no one come to rescue me?*

I couldn't hold back the tears any longer, and I just fell apart. Sobbing, in that nasty, snotty way. The absolutely, unattractive kind of despair. The kind that leaves you with red eyes and snot running from your nose. Collapsing onto the cold floor, in utter desolation.

For once this was so unexpected, apparently, that Charles just stood there, staring. Then he hauled me up and dragged me to the bed. Before I knew it, I was in the bed, manacled with the covers over me as I watched his back disappear out the door.

Eventually, I began to calm down. Curling myself up as small as I can, I tried and get some warmth.

Before long he reappeared with the food he promised earlier, dry toast yet again and a paper cup of water. He didn't speak, just placed it on the floor and vanished again out the door.

This time I didn't wait. I reached over and quickly downed the food and drink before he could change his mind, and take it away from me. *It seems nothing I do is right, so I might as well chance it.*

I managed to get a little warmth back in my body, and eventually fell into a fitful sleep.

I jumped as I open my eyes to find Charles stood over me. Watching me sleep. *Creepy*, I think.

"Good. You are finally awake. I have the paperwork ready. I will allow you upstairs so that you can sign it and then you may have a bath if you behave yourself, slut," he snapped. "I have wasted enough time."

My manacle undone, and leash attached, I crawled out of bed. Every inch of me was now sore, and aching. A bath sounded wonderful right now, I decided.

The kitchen was bright as we enter, the snow outside reflecting the light. *Daytime again. Did that make this four days, or five now? I am so confused with the passage of time. I wonder where the girl that served us is? I only saw her that once. Maybe, she doesn't live here.* Then I breathed in a glorious smell. Someone had been cooking biscuits in the kitchen. I could smell a mixture of vanilla, chocolate and coffee. *Maybe, she is here somewhere after all. I simply can't imagine Charles cooking biscuits.*

We moved on through to the dining room again, and a pot of tea was set there. Milk, sugar and even a small plate of those chocolate chip cookies I could smell were set out, e

nticingly. Who knew that biscuits could smell so good. The room was warm and there was a waft of Potpourri in the air. Roses, I thought. The smell of mould and mildew in the cellar overwhelmed any other smell there might be down there.

I could also smell Charles. Soap, and aftershave. The aftershave was too pungent. Overpowering. All it did was remind me of Simon, and Alistair. Just how amazing they both smelled.

Charles picked up the silver bell, and rang it twice. Again, the young girl appeared. All she was wearing today was an apron, with cherries on. Nothing more. She put milk in the cups and then looked at me for the first time and said. "Coffee, or tea Miss?" with a cockney accent.

"Tea, please." I responded.

She didn't ask Charles, just poured him a coffee, with two lumps of sugar and pushed it toward him with great care. Bending over so that I could see her bare arse and the fresh stripes on them. Red and raised. Seems I was not the only one he hit.

"Sugar, Miss?" she asked.

"No, thanks." I replied. *Jesus, you would think we were in a tea room, with all this. Not me naked and her virtually so.*

"Drink your tea, Sweetness." Charles insisted. "Before it gets cold."

I picked up the cup, gratefully nursing it in my hands, which were still icy cold. The warmth of the cup spread welcome heat into my fingers.

"Biscuit, Miss?" Little Miss Cockney asked.

"Thanks." I replied, picking up two at once. That was, until I saw Charles' raised eyebrows.

I put one back, and nibbled on the remaining one.

I felt like Alice at the Mad Hatter's tea party. This was such a peculiar scene unfolding here.

"You are dismissed, Sweetness," he told the girl, and she quickly vanished again. But to where, I had no clue.

Charles watched me over the papers he was examining. He waited until I had had a final sip of my tea and finished my cookie. Then he moved all the dishes and cups to the side.

He placed the paperwork down in front of me. The first was a non-disclosure contract. *Not unheard of in a Dom/sub relationship. Accepted, even.* The next document was thicker, and I presumed it to be the contract he wished me to sign. Technically, it would not be binding. No D/s contract truly can be. But, incriminating all the same if I put my signature on it, as I would then be consenting to all he would do to me. The last, I assumed, was a copy of the slave registration. A number is given, and slaves often have this tattooed or branded onto them. Or it can be on their slave collars.

I signed the non-disclosure agreement quickly. There wasn't much to read and it was like all the others I had signed previously. I stopped for a moment and pondered. And, like the one I should have been signing right now for Simon, and Alistair. I heard Charles clear his throat, and I started to read through the contract.

He had my soft, and hard limits there. I then realised that this document had probably been prepared for some time. This was what he expected all along. I checked the date and it was from the day that I blocked him. I studied it in more detail. He had actually altered some of my hard limits. He now had a couple as soft limits, instead. I looked up and into his eyes. His eyes narrowed, he knew I had spotted the discrepancy.

I carried on reading, and then I saw it already mentioned the slave register. My gut feeling was right. He never wanted a sub, but a slave. I checked the slave registration and sure enough, the number is the same. *Shit. This was his plan, all along. To make me his 24/7 slave.* My nervousness increased.

Then I read the next part. I was to have the slave number branded to a specific part of my body. A very tender part.

The door-bell rang, and I startled at the sound. *Oh, my God. Someone is at the door. Maybe I can ask them for help?* Then I noticed Charles' reaction, or should I say, lack of it. *It must be someone he knows for him to be so calm and collected.*

Just then the Little Cockney Miss appeared again. This time she was not alone. The dark-haired man stood next to her was huge. Despite having a jumper on, tattoos were clearly visible, all over his neck and hands. He was carrying a large brown leather holdall.

"Joe is here, Sir." And with a little curtsey off she went again.

I tried to cover up with the papers I held, but to no avail.

From Willing Sub To Enslaved Captive

Joe nodded to Charles then turned his gaze upon me. Weighing me up instantly.

"Is this the one that needs the brand? Virgin skin too, by the looks of it. No tattoos? No piercings either, I imagine. Well, that is, until today. Lucky girl."

Piercings! What the fuck is that all about? I wondered and I looked back at the paperwork and there, in black and white, I saw exactly what he meant.

Underneath the reference to the branding, was an addition paragraph, detailing the piercings that were to grace my body. Both nipples, and my labia were to be pierced. My labia were to be pierced, three times. There was even a little sodding diagram of what would be done to me. *Over my dead fucking body, it would. No fucker is going to brand, or pierce anything without my say so.*

I looked up in disgust, and more than a little terror and saw Charles' expression. I had played straight into his hands. He had mentioned the piercings in passing when we were together, and I had told him in no uncertain terms that that, would never happen. Not in a month of Sundays. He always intended it to happen. With, or without my permission, apparently. The smug look on the bastards' face, said it all.

As I was reading, Joe must have moved closer as the next thing I knew he said to Charles. "May I?" with a nod toward me and I saw Charles nod YES.

He reached over and grabbed my nipples, squeezing them hard enough to make me hiss.

"What the actual fuck?" I shouted. I had enough of this shit. The penny finally dropped. Nothing I did, or appeared to do to be compliant, would make a jot of difference to my situation. Charles intended to punish me whenever, and however he wanted. My being a willing participant, or not, was irrelevant to him.

The worm was about to turn, and I would fight them every step of the way. No matter the outcome. If he carried on with the lack of food and drink and my remaining in that fucking cellar, I would be dead soon enough anyway. So, I decided it was time to fight back.

"This one's a feisty one, Charles." Joe said. "Should make the branding and piercing pretty interesting. Are we going to tie the little bitch up?"

"Don't worry. I can always drug her. We have done that before too." Charles replied.

Shit. I'm definitely not the first. What happened to the others, then? I thought. Are all bloody Doms psychic? Because that was when I was to be taught a lesson. Charles rang the bell and when Miss Cockney appeared he asked her to bring the *others* in.

Before long, she returned accompanied by two other girls. All pretty and young. One had dark brown hair and looked a little Hispanic, with her sallow skin. The other had long black hair and almond shaped, chocolate brown eyes. They all stood to attention in the present position, eyes down.

"Girls. This is our latest recruit, Suzie. You will all refer to her as Slut though. At least until she learns her place. Now then, Suzie is apparently unhappy about having her piercings and branding done. I think she should see just how beautiful they are. Maybe that will help to change her mind. She can see your nipples easily and when I say turn. I want you to turn around and show her your brands and piercings. Understand, my sweet things?"

A chorus of "Yes, Sir," followed, and my eyes were drawn to their breasts and the nipple piercings each girl wore. Not only that, some had weights attached to the nipples. Heavy ones by the look of it.

"Turn, now." He commanded and as one, they turned and bent over, so that I could admire not only the piercings they all wore, but the brands that had been burnt into their bottoms.

As with the nipple piercings, some had weights attached, and one girl had her pussy completely closed, using the piercings to hold them together. All this did was fuel the fire I had, to not have any of these atrocities done without my permission. Okay, I had considered having my nipples pierced at some time in the future. But, nobody was going to decide for me. It was my body, after all.

At that I turned and walked to the table. Snatching the contracts one by one I tore them all in half.

"No," was all I said. It was all I needed to say.

CHAPTER 19

Charles erupted from his chair and slapped me hard across the face. Temper well and truly lost, he dragged me out of the dining room and towards the stairs. The girls parted ranks quickly with terrified looks on all their faces.

I was virtually thrown down the stairs and shortly found myself once more manacled to the bed.

I cowered down, refusing to look up.

"So, you, are too good for me, are you? Too good to be my slave? Or wear my brand and my piercings? We'll see about that, shall we? You will wear my brand if I have to drug you, and tie you down. The same for the piercings. You are mine now, Slut. No one is going to come charging in here this time to save your sorry arse. No one knows or cares where you are. Maybe it is time you just accept that and make it easier on both of us."

He turned and slammed out of the cellar, stamping up the stairs.

Shit, I have done it now I thought as I lay there, unmoving.

I had no clue how much time had passed since I had been dragged to the cellar but it was quite some time. I managed to grab a drink in the paper cup I still had and knew I had to drink more after I peed and it was dark brown in colour. Not a good colour for pee at the best of times. If nothing else I needed to keep hydrated. I kept looking up at the cameras. I could feel his eyes on me.

How the hell has he got away with all those girls being here? Is there no one out there looking for them? No other friends or relatives? How long have they been here? I simply couldn't get my head around it. *Come to think of it. What were all those scars on his back about? Plenty of people have a ton of crap in their lives, it doesn't make them do it to others.*

The waiting was getting to me. My angst increasing, the longer I lay there. I alternated between wanting him to come and get whatever he was going to do, over with, and being scared shitless at the thought of what he might do. I had no clue what he was capable of. Was he capable of murder? Who knew?

I roused from my pondering, as I heard footsteps approaching the door to the cellar. His footsteps. I knew them well by now. I had no clue what to do. *Do I stand up to present position? Or not? I think he will make it clear to me, what he wants me to do.* Fear gripped me as I waited there with bated breath. *Do I obey him? Or not?* Indecision slammed into me.

He opened the door, slowly. No slamming this time. He was in control right now. He obviously knew exactly what he was doing.

He walked in. My breathing speeded up my heart racing as my muscles tightened. Fight, or flight.

Palms damp, as the stress starts to kick in.

The look in his eyes, pure evil.

Despite his baby-faced charm his face hardened. Eyes slitted, as he regarded me with a sneer.

He grabbed at the covers and threw them across the room. Then he leaned over and grabbed at my breasts with brutal force. Taking my breath away, as I howled in pain.

"It's time you knew who was boss here. The Master. These," he squeezed again, as I once more shrieked in pain, "are mine. Every fucking hole is mine. Every part of you is mine. You will understand that very soon. I won't allow you to disobey me. Do you understand? Slut?"

I nodded as best I could, unable to articulate the simplest words. I gritted my teeth as he proceeded to pull me to stand with the grip on my breasts. They felt afire, as if he could somehow pull them clean off my body.

He let go and I grabbed at them, just holding them, with tears in my eyes. Meanwhile, he had unfastened the manacle and I saw the gag in his hand. My eyes went wide. *Why would he need a gag if no one can hear me in here? What was he going to do to me that was so bad, so awful?*

The gag was forced into my mouth, and fastened. His strength seemed to be multiplied by the sheer explosive anger I felt from him. As I struggled to escape, I spotted the ropes he had on his belt. He was so quick that before I knew it, he had me tied up, securely. The rope was secured to chains hanging down from the suspension hook. My hands were stretched above my head and fastened to a suspension ring from the ceiling. He pulled sharply, and I had no option but to stand on my tip toes.

He picked up a spreader bar from the rack on the wall and fastened my feet to either side. Then secured this to ties in the floor.

He checked the ties, and then walked over to the rack of whips and canes, and stood there for a while. Whatever he was about to use on me, was on that rack.

He reached over and selected something, but I couldn't be sure what. Then I saw it. It was a single tailed whip. And it looked familiar, somehow.

He came back to stand in front of me. He punched me in the face, his fist slamming into my jaw with force. "Sweetheart, we are going to have such a good time. Aren't we?"

I shook my head wildly and tried to scream around my gag. Throwing my head from side to side to no avail. Unable to escape any further hits.

He ran the single-tail through his hands, lovingly. Sliding it through his fingers like a lover.

My eyes were streaming and my face on fire.

Leaning in again so that I cringed in anticipation of his next move, he snatched my head back with a fistful of hair.

"Do you remember when we last saw each other, my Sweet? In the sex shop? I was buying this for you, then."

He held the single-tail up closer so that I could see that it had been altered in some way. The ends now had a tiny metal chain attached to them.

"In fact, I had it especially adapted for you. To enhance it." Cocking his head slightly, he watched my face.

Abruptly he stepped back, letting go of my hair. My scalp stung in response, bringing fresh tears to my eyes.

I blinked them away, as I tried to focus, and work out his next move.

A feeling of dread overcame over me, as slithers of ice seemed to run through my veins. My nipples pebbling in response. Goosebumps formed, as all the tiny hairs on my body quickly stood to attention. Not in anticipation of pleasure, but overwhelming terror. Mortal fear.

My heart jackhammered in my chest, thrumming so loud that I could hear the rushing in my ears. Surely, he would be able to hear it, too.

Stopping in front of me, so close, he leaned into me, trailing a finger gently along my jaw, towards my lips.

"Bitch."

The sound of the backhand slap he gave me ricocheted loudly around the room as my head was thrown sharply to the left.

"Slut."

Crack! The noise was deafening as he connected with my left cheek.

He began to circle me, walking slowly. A predator, weighing up his prey. I could feel his eyes burning into me. Examining me closely. Stopping and touching. Although the touches were soft and gentle, I cringed each time, whimpering through the ball-gag.

"What a beautiful canvas. Your soft creamy flesh. I will paint you with welts and bruises. You will be a work of art. MY work of art."

Terrified, I started to shiver. *He's mad. Completely loco. Off his head. Oh, my God what is he going to do to me?*

Then, in the blink of an eye, he struck. Hard.

The single tail lashed my shoulder. The strike hurt immensely, but the aftermath was stronger and lingered.

The air was expelled from my lungs as I tried to draw in another breath.

Just as I managed to do that he struck again, harder this time. I could now feel the first hit throb, and I felt something wet begin to ooze. It dawned on me that he had broken the skin already. It was blood that was beginning to run down my shoulder and down my back.

He struck again. The hits slowly working down my body and travelling towards my breasts. The pain was overwhelming, blossoming and growing with each subsequent hit.

The fourth hit caught the bottom half of my breast and the blood sprayed out. Sending rivulets of blood down over my ribs and side. Then, I heard the first splat as the blood began to drip, drip and hit the floor.

Despite my pain, I looked down and reeled in shock at the sight before me. A small pool of blood was gathering. I began to panic and fight against my bonds.

Yet another strike hit. Further up towards the nipple. My thrashing was now causing the chains above me to rattle and clank. The pain was searing, the intensity overwhelming. The force he was using escalated with each hit.

Drool flew from my gag, spraying spittle and blood alike. My jaw clenched around the gag in earnest.

He stopped. "The next strike, my Sweet, will split the nipple. Let's see how sensitive your nipples will be when I have split them both. After today you won't be able to have your nipples pierced. It won't be physically possible. Your choice, my sweet of course. You refused my marks. I am sure you will be happy for me to soothe them later. In fact, you will be begging me to," he seethed.

I raised my head, wild eyed at this remark. *What the fuck*! I had an awful sinking feeling that this was only the beginning.

I watched as he raised his arm, concentrating hard on his next strike as the door to the dungeon exploded open and Simon and Alistair stampeded through.

Unfortunately, not in time to stop the strike altogether, but enough to cause Charles to falter a little. The strike missing its mark by mere centimetres. As the skin on the underside of my breast split apart. Blood flying through the air.

Alistair rugby-tackled Charles as Simon rushed over towards me stricken.

If I wasn't being held up by the ropes I would have hit the deck.

In moments Simon had me free and was gently cradling me, carrying me to the iron bed. Snagging the sheets as makeshift bandages. Stemming the flow of blood as best he could.

I was struggling to stay conscious. I could hear Simon's voice repeating. "Stay with me baby. Just stay with me. I've got you. We've got you now."

I could hear, as if a long way away, the struggle that Alistair was having.

"Al, grab the rope and tie him up. Fasten him to the god damned rig that he had Suzie fastened to. To secure him. The police are on their way. They should be here any minute now. You are one lucky bastard, Charles. If I hadn't have taken my Hippocratic oath, you would be a dead man. That, and Al can't be tainted with killing a man. Otherwise you would be fucking dead by now."

I could then hear Simon on the phone to someone. From the conversation, it sounded strangely like a plastic surgeon. Then all hell broke loose again as the police appeared, asking about the three naked girls upstairs.

Charles was snarling as they cuffed him, and led him away as he shouted back to us all. "You think you have won, don't you? You haven't. I will get what is mine back, if it's the last thing I do. She is mine. That bitch is mine. They all are." His voice faded into the distance, as he was dragged off to the police station.

The police would need statements from all of us, but first I needed some medical treatment. *I am so weary*, I thought. *I just need to sleep in a warm bed, for starters. Something nice to eat would be good, too.*

Paramedics arrived, and after examining my wounds they loaded me onto a stretcher. I was not being taken to the local A & E, but to a private hospital. I was correct about the fact that I would need a plastic surgeon. My injuries were now covered in dressings, so I accepted this is the best course of action. I had no intention of arguing with a doctor who was also my Dom. Not a wise move.

Simon travelled with me in the ambulance, with Alistair following in the car. I fell asleep on my way there, with Simon stroking my hair. I must have imagined it, but I was sure I saw him wiping his eyes. As if he was crying. My mind was a whirl, as I tried to come to terms with what had happened in the last five days.

Before long we arrived at the hospital. Claire, my mum and dad, were already there. They had been frantic, trying to find me. Claire and my mum were crying, and Dad looked teary-eyed too. But I was his little girl, even at my age.

"Lamb, we were so worried about you." Mum began "We were beside ourselves. Luckily Claire found your address book back at the flat, and was able to contact Dad and me. The boys got in touch with us, too. They have been going out of their minds trying to work out where that madman took you. I'm still trying to come to terms with the fact that our little girl has two boyfriends, though. I must admit, that one of them would be enough for me."

I felt myself blush. I couldn't believe they knew about our arrangement. *How will I ever live this down? Mum and Dad are so... normal.*

Simon and Alistair arrived, bringing coffees and teas for everyone. I, though, was not allowed anything to drink as I had an IV running with fluids. I couldn't argue with the reasoning, as I was due to go down to theatre for surgery shortly. The surgeon, a friend of Simon's had been to see me and I had had my pre-op assessment so it wouldn't be long, now. He was a lovely guy and, surprise, surprise, another Dom.

"We thought we would never find you, Suzie, but then we tried a trace on your phone and bingo. It was in the back of a taxi cab, with a very guilty looking taxi driver unable to explain why it was there. He is now at Her Majesty's pleasure. Some people will do about anything for money. That, and we had help from the police and a private detective. We were leaving nothing to chance. The house you were being kept prisoner in, was inherited and registered to Charles, about five years ago. So, we decided to check it out and spotted Charles' car in the driveway. The most confusing thing was the three naked girls that ran around screaming when we rang the doorbell. We presumed they were expecting the person at the door to be someone they knew," Simon explained.

Alistair took up the story. "Once we had the taxi driver, and a description of the kidnapper, it was pretty easy to put two and two together. How are you feeling, Pet?" With that Alistair leaned over and kissed me. Simon followed suit. Mum's face was a picture and Claire just giggled, nearly spitting her coffee all over the floor in the process.

"Not too bad, thanks, considering the last five days. I will be glad when I can have something decent to eat and drink, though. Porridge is so overrated, "I quipped, trying to hold it together for everyone.

Simon was having none of it, though. "Hey. You don't need to put a brave face on it, Sweetheart. That imbecile hurt you badly. I wanted you to have the best. That is why I contacted the best cosmetic surgeon I know. His microsurgery techniques will leave minimal scarring to the places that Charles struck you with the single tail. I can't believe how much weight you have lost. You are all skin and bones. We will have to spoil you, and feed you up. "

I felt myself welling up and, before long, the waterworks had started again. Everyone took turns holding and hugging me. I was so weary, now. The nurse and porter arrived and, after a quick check, I was on my way to theatre. Simon insisting on escorting me to the entrance of the theatre and holding my hand. To be honest, I was glad he did as I was not feeling very safe now. *I think it will be a long time before I feel safe anywhere again for a long, long time.*

I turned my head to watch him until the doors closed. Soon I was being prepped. All the staff were lovely, and knew about my ordeal. The nurse even held my hand, until I was under the anaesthetic.

I awoke feeling very groggy, and very disorientated. Luckily, I had Simon, and Alistair sat either side of me. They had insisted on taking Mum, Dad and Claire home, as they were pretty much exhausted after so many days of worrying about me.

Dr White, the surgeon who had operated on me called by, and told me how the op had gone. He reassured me that any scarring would be minimal, and that using scar management we could reduce that further. I just had to wait for the scabs to fall off, and I could begin the regime. For the most part, the rest of my injuries were mainly bruising and welts. Lots of bruising. Each time I moved I regretted it.

The only other concern he had was my mental health after my ordeal. I tried to make out it wouldn't be a problem. But there was no fooling him. I was jumping at the least noise, and my heartrate soared at the slightest thing. Perhaps a visit or two, to a counsellor wouldn't go amiss.

Being a sub, I already knew what a great help arnica cream would be. So, I insisted that one of my Doms go and buy some from the pharmacy, nearby. They were falling over each other for the opportunity to rub it in. I told them both off for making me laugh. It hurt when I laughed. I might be allowed home the following day. It depended how well I recovered from the surgery and what the blood tests said. I did have a doctor on call at home after all, but I had a feeling that Simon might be quite strict, if he thought I wasn't up to returning home straight away. I turned to them, and asked. "When is Christmas Eve? I have lost track, now."

"Today is Tuesday, and Christmas Eve is this Friday. So, only three days away." Alistair replied.

"But I haven't got any presents for anyone. I need to buy presents." Weepy once again, I promptly burst into tears. *Flaming heck. Is this all I can do now? Cry at the least thing? What's wrong with me?*

I must have repeated the last bit out loud, as I got told that I had all the time in the world to come to terms with what happened. That it was perfectly normal to be disorientated, and upset after my imprisonment.

I finally got something to eat but they started me off with something light, as I had hardly eaten for five days and my stomach had shrunk quite a bit. I couldn't eat all of it so just as well.

Simon and Alistair decided that the only way they would be happy, was if both stayed with me overnight that night. If I had to stop longer, they would take it in turns.

I didn't tell them, but, I was so happy with this decision. As I wasn't sure that I could even fall asleep. I was anxious and flinching at the least thing. I wasn't even sure I would be able to sleep with them there, but I thought it was more likely if they were there to protect me.

The porter brought in an extra day bed. It wasn't unusual to have relatives to stay over. Simon nipped out to ring his mum and dad, and explain what was happening. They were going to come and visit me tomorrow. This prospect made me more than a little anxious.

The lights went down and both of my men were settled. One either side of my bed, like sentinels. I had some pain relief, my IV antibiotics were administered and arnica cream was massaged into my bruises once again.

It was now time to sleep.

I lay there for hours. If I heard one of them move, I closed my eyes. There was no point in us all being awake. Finally, exhausted, I slipped into an uneasy sleep. Then the nightmares began. In them, I was back in the cellar, my prison. Charles was doing more, and more bizarre and unusual torture on me. Piercings, everywhere. Branding my body, until there was no skin left without a brand. It went on, and on, endlessly until I began to scream.

I awoke with Simon's and Alistair's arms wrapped about me. A cocoon of love, and safety. Sobbing hysterically, I was unable to stop at first, until they stroked and kissed me and I found solace in their arms.

Simon shushed me back to sleep with whispers of safety and love. Telling me it was early days and that we would come through this, together.

The one thing I knew, was their love was the source of my recovery. They would help me be whole again.

ABOUT THE AUTHOR

SCARLETT FLAME

I am passionate about writing, and write about passion. I am a qualified Children's Nurse, and have a degree and Pg. Dip (Masters qualification), so probably not someone you would expect to write erotica. Although born in Salford, I reside in Manchester, England. I gave up nursing in October 2014, in order to concentrate fully on writing. I love to read and write, but only started writing seriously in 2012. Music is important to me and this is why you are likely to find me attending gigs, and enjoying the Indie bands that abound in Manchester.

As an avid reader and writer, I share reviews of books, gigs, album reviews and interviews on my blog.

I hope you enjoyed my book and I would love to hear from you.

OTHER BOOKS BY SCARLETT FLAME

BOUND FOR PASSION: EROTIC LOVE STORIES

by
Scarlett Flame
Copyright © 2013 Scarlett Flame

When Vivienne sits inconsolable in the hospital chapel, the last encounter she expects is a fervent entanglement with an otherworldly being. As passions increase, she learns for the first time in her life the true meaning of out of this world. In the second, Sarah meets a new lover, after telling him all her intimate fantasies in an internet chat room. And, the final story concerns the journey a young woman takes, as a Dominant offers to show her the ropes, in exchange for her submission via BDSM. Individually these stories are hot, but together they are sizzling.

THE VISIT

EXCERPT

We had met on the internet. You know, in a chat room, and arranged to meet up.

The plane had just landed, and I was extremely nervous, but excited. The things we had discussed online had made my heart race, so many fantasies that we had both had. Now that we were meeting up, maybe, hopefully, some of those fantasies would be fulfilled.

I stood waiting at the luggage carousel, until I spotted my suitcase. The red satin ribbon I'd tied on the handle now seemed like a little flag.

I'd dressed in a slim fitting black pencil skirt, scarlet top and scarlet suede high heel shoes. My underwear was especially chosen with him in mind. A black lacy bra, a new black lacy thong, finished off with stockings and suspenders. A short black leather jacket over the top created the look.

Even when I'd retrieved my case, I loitered a few minutes longer by the carousel, wondering what would happen when we met. Would I even recognise him? We had seen pictures of each other, and he'd heard my voice. I knew he was over six-foot tall, and he knew I was a little over five foot five inches, so he would be taller than me.

My hands were sweating a little now, and my legs were shaking too. Would I be able to go through with this? Would he? I nipped to the toilets, my nervousness making me need a pee. I brushed my hair and reapplied my make-up, staring at my reflection.

I left the toilets, making my way slowly through the double doors in to the airport foyer. With my eyes firmly trained on my feet, worrying that I might trip, or fall, or do something stupid. Suddenly, I felt his gaze, and I just knew it was him. When I raised my head, and our eyes met, I spotted him straight away. There he was. Tall, dark, and handsome, and headed my way. It might have been cliché, but it was true, and he was mine, for the entire weekend.

My throat hurt now, and my heart stuttered in my chest. I stood stock still. As if my feet were suddenly encased in concrete, I couldn't move. He didn't falter, but instead gathered me up in his arms, then he was kissing me. A long, lingering kiss. The sort of kiss you never want to end. I dropped my bag and let go of my suitcase, oblivious to anyone who may have been watching.

When he began to speak, I detected the amazing Irish lilt I knew he would have, and I just melted, well it felt that way to me. He picked up my suitcase and took my hand saying "I'm so glad you are here. My friend is going to drop us off at the hotel we are staying at. Come on, I can't wait for us to be alone."

We left the airport hand in hand and walked to the short stay car park. I could see a little white fiesta with a blond-haired guy in the driver's seat. Paul waved, and the guy got out and opened the boot. Paul put my suitcase in, next to a large holdall, and we both climbed in to the back of the car.

We sat there, not speaking, just holding hands, staring out of the window. The town was lovely and quaint, with the houses painted all different colours, but my eyes kept drifting back to Paul. He began to speak immediately,

"We're almost there now. This is Michael, by the way. We're meeting up with him and a few other friends later on

tonight." Michael glanced over his shoulder at me and added "Hi, nice to meet you" Paul inched a little closer, our thighs touching now. I could feel the heat of his body through his jeans.

Michael pulled the car up to the front of a fairly nondescript hotel, called The Mermaid. Paul and I got out, he retrieved the suitcase and holdall, and we said our goodbyes to Michael.

As we walked in to the hotel, I began to think about the first fantasy we had discussed, and could feel my face begin to flush. We approached the front desk and signed in, picking up our keys in the process. The Concierge enquired whether we needed someone to show us to our room. Paul replied, "No, thanks, we can manage," and we headed toward the lifts, opposite the desk. When he turned to me, his smile was more of a grin. "You ready to take the lift, Sarah?"

I gulped, and nodded. My mouth was too dry to speak now, as if it was full of sand. We got into the lift, and the doors closed with a whoosh.

Immediately Paul had me pinned against the side wall of the lift, indicating over his shoulder to the camera blinking in the corner. "You remember what we discussed?" Before I could respond he leaned in to me, kissing me deeply, ferociously. His hands wandered down toward the hem of my skirt and continued their journey up the inside of my thigh.

By now my new thong was wet, as I remembered exactly what our "discussion" had been about.

Discussion about a fantasy involving a lift, and what we would do there. With his free hand, he pressed the "stop" button for the lift. Reaching his fingers into either side of my panties, he eased them slowly down, until he was knelt at my feet, and I was able to step out of them. He brought them up to his nose, sniffed deeply, and slipped them in to his jeans pocket, all the time making sure that the camera was recording everything. I was aroused, and embarrassed at the same time. Once again, his hands travelled up the inside of my thigh. This time he inserted two fingers and gasped. "So, wet, I knew you would love this. Just wait till we get to the room. I will rock your world."

BOUND FOR PASSION

AVAILABLE ON AMAZON NOW.

A VALENTINE'S BIND

Manchester Dominants and submissive's book 1.
When University student Nicky Johnson decides to make
an impromptu visit to a BDSM club with friends, she gets
more than she bargained for.
The alcohol fuelled evening finds her asleep on her sofa
the next day, suffering from memory loss.
But who brought her home?
Dominant Dariel Pearson shows her that spanking and
submission can be empowering.
Will this be a life changing experience for Nicky?
Available on Amazon now.
This New Adult contemporary romance is a steamy, sexy
tale of love, dominance and submission.

NICKY

I woke up slowly. Opening first one eye then the other tentatively. My head banging and my mouth felt like the bottom of a parrot cage. The need for food immediate and overpowering. The mantra in my head repeating over and over.

I am never drinking red wine again. I am never drinking red wine again.

Then, I spotted the open packets and containers of food spread across the coffee table in the living room. No wonder my neck hurt so much. Falling asleep on the sofa with my head at an unnatural angle will do that to a person.

With a selection of leftovers heated up I began munching aimlessly. Trying to remember how I got home the previous evening. And, the twenty-dollar question was "Who with?" I could hear someone coming through my front door with a key.

But, I lived alone, and no one else had keys to my flat. Not even my family.

I turned to look as the handle started to twist, panicking as the door pushed open, and in stepped a stunning man with dark brown hair. He was wearing, what looked to me like a Saville Row suit. His steely blue gaze connecting with my own slightly bloodshot pale blue eyes.

"Oh. Finally, awake, are we?" he remarked in a clipped accent as he walked in shutting the door carefully behind him.

I attempted to swallow the mouthful of curry I was in the middle of chewing, and began to cough violently. It had gone down the wrong hole and I was turning an unattractive blue hue.

Reacting quickly, he shot over and banged me on the back sharply three times, dislodging the errant bit of curry. Which promptly shot out of my mouth, landing on the rug.

Oh. My God. How embarrassing.

I didn't have a clue who he was, and this is how he gets his first glimpse of me. Eating warmed up curry.

Looking like, I had been dragged backwards through a hedge. Except, apparently, this wasn't our first meeting at all. He had a key to my flat and seemed to know his way around.

What on earth went on last night?

Grabbing some tissues, I cleaned up the mess on the rug, and guiltily started to tidy up the living area. He grabbed my arm firmly, turned me to face him and commanded.

"Stop that right now. We need to talk. Sit down there."

He pointed to the sofa and I felt an overwhelming compulsion to follow his orders.

"Right. Tell me what you remember from last night. The truth mind you. I won't be lied to."

I opened my mouth, then closed it again. This happened a few times, as I had no idea what did happen, how he came to have a key, or even how I got home.

"Enough of that now. You look like a demented goldfish, opening and closing your mouth like that. So, I assume from your body language and failure to respond that you haven't a clue who I am. No idea what I am doing here, or even aware of the fact I had to escort you home?"

I nodded and shrugged. Not trusting myself to talk without making the situation worse. So, the "who" I came home with was revealed.

"Well then. Perhaps introductions are in order. For starters, I know a little about you already. Your name is Nicola Johnson, or Nicky to your friends. You are a student at Salford University studying sociology, who works in a bar in town part-time. Your parents live in Spain having retired recently. Are you sure you can't remember anything about yesterday evening?" He Quizzed. A stern look on his face.

I STARED at him and tried my absolute best to remember something, anything. He did look familiar, but I couldn't even remember his name, where we had met, or what had led to us coming home together. He wasn't even my type, which was the big shocker. He looked way to sophisticated for a piss poor student like me to snaffle.

"Well...I remember your face. But, other than that it is hazy. I must have drunk way too much red wine last night to blank out the entire evening like this." I replied.

"Oh, petal I think the shots might have something to do with the memory loss. That, and the spliff I found you sharing with the guys that wanted to take you home with them. For a threesome, as I remember rightly."

THE PROPHECY UNFOLDS

(DRAGON QUEEN)

Life is not measured by the breaths you take, but by the
moments that take your breath away - Anon.

Synopsis

For Alex, this was supposed to be a fresh start.
New job, new part of the country. But she got much more
than she bargained for.
As she travelled through the Snowdonia National park,
with its remote villages and Wales' highest mountains, she
stops to eat a bite of lunch. There she is kidnapped by three
strangers, and transported to the Dystopian, Steampunk
world of Syros.
A world of dragons, magic and werewolves. Where
science fiction, meets science fact. This is only the beginning
of an epic urban fantasy, and the fulfilment of a prophecy
over 200 years old.
Will she survive on a planet where three factions battle
for dominance?

Book One of the series Dragon Queen

EXCERPT

CHAPTER ONE

Finally, my life was getting back on track following a worrisome number of months.

I had had a great deal of trouble sleeping of late. I had been constantly disturbed by dreams I can only describe as nightmares!

These dreams always included the same shadowy characters with obscure faces. The one recurring theme being, I became intimate with each one of them. To say this wasn't in my usual nature would be an understatement.

In all my relationships, I had always been monogamous. Fundamentally a one-man-girl, who wouldn't dream of being unfaithful. Perhaps, because of this, these dreams proved very disturbing and included sexual acts I'd heard of, but would never think of taking part in. Little did I suspect that these dreams would prove to be the precursor to an amazing series of adventures.

The story proper began one-day while driving through the glorious Welsh countryside on my way to check out accommodations procured in anticipation of my move. This would act as a base to work from Monday to Friday, at my new job.

Previously, I had worked in a general hospital close to my family home in Manchester. But I wanted to spread my wings after ending a long-term relationship with my childhood sweetheart, Paul.

I realised that I now needed space to develop new friendships, and put my love life on the back burner. My career would become my first priority. So, this became part of that plan. My new contract was as a Children's Nurse for an Agency in a hospital not far from Bangor in North Wales, which meant relocating.

On that day, I drove through Snowdonia National Park, where pine trees crowded either side of the road. I spotted a little picnic area to one side, flanked by a small car park. It was a beautiful sunny day and as I had brought along a packed lunch, I parked up to take advantage of the sunny weather. As I parked I realised mine was the only car there, but thought no more about it. I had no problem eating here at the edge of the forest

I retrieved my sandwich, carton of orange juice, and my book as I wandered over to the farthest table. From here it was possible to watch the squirrels and birds as they searched amongst the bins for crumbs.

I'd sat there enjoying my book for about ten minutes, when two things happened. First, I became aware that a hush had descended suddenly in the forest. I no longer heard the scampering of the squirrels or the birds singing. When I looked up, I couldn't see any of them around the area they had occupied only a few minutes earlier.

The second thing was a sound that I could only compare to that of the sound barrier being broken. A whoosh, bang, and a slight popping noise. Yet an instant after, the birds and squirrels returned, chirping and moving through the grass as before.

I shrugged, went back to the page in my book, and continued to eat. However, after a while a sense of uneasiness descended over me. I raised my head to find myself being spied upon.

The watcher, a tall broad-shouldered man with dirty blond hair tied at the nape. His eyes were the most vivid blue I had ever beheld. I estimated him to be about twenty-five to thirty years old. He regarded me with silent intensity. His odd clothing caught my eye. Old fashioned garments, dark trousers laced up the front, a long-sleeved suede jacket of a similar material, and leather boots.

I turned my head to check for any cars or vans in the car park, then jumped as I spotted two more men. One to my left, and another I saw in my peripheral vision to the right.

The man on the left appeared to be dressed similar to the first, but with sandy hair and sea-green eyes.

In contrast, he wasn't quite as broad, although equally tall. All three men appeared over six feet tall. The last had dark hair to his shoulders that hung loose, and I saw the most amazing violet eyes.

The appearance of these men with no noise, and staring at me in rapt fascination not uttering a word, spooked me. My heart began beating so loud and fast I thought that I was having some kind of heart attack.

But, the most unnerving thing of all was, all three men appeared familiar, a déjà vu sort of moment. I'd dreamt about these three men for so long. I knew at once these were the shady characters from my dreams. Dreams that time after time had haunted my sleep over the last year.

I decided that sitting still was stupid, so made a grab for my bag and shot through to the right as I ran toward one of the many footpaths I'd spotted earlier.

My flight or fight response gave me swift feet, (or so I thought), but obviously not swift enough. Before I got ten yards down the path two of the three had already moved, appearing in front of me. Shifting so fast I could hardly believe my eyes. I turned to head back to where I'd come from, hoping to make it back to my car.

Fate once again took charge, as I ran straight into the third man, the blond. It was like running into a brick wall, as he ensnared me in his solid muscular arms. My heart stuttered, and I felt the zing of an electric current pass through my body. I never claimed to be a particularly brave person, and I hyperventilated, gasping, as I endeavoured to catch my breath.

One of them began to stroke my hair, saying,

"Calm down Alex, calm down. Breathe slowly, we won't hurt you," but, at that point my knees gave way and I collapsed into darkness, terrified.

How did he know my name was Alex?

I came to, lay on a huge bed in a strange bedroom – the biggest bed I'd ever seen. Enormous! All that came to mind was a little rhyme my granddad used to sing, "Ten in the bed and the little one said roll over", it was so big. The other thing I noticed, was the odd lighting. The fixtures resembled gas lamps of some sort, but were giving off normal light. Candles set either side of the bed were obviously not there as a decoration, because they were all burnt down with use. How strange everything appeared.

Sitting on the bed next to me, to my right, was the sandy haired man from the car park. To my left, the one with dark hair, while standing at the end of the bed was the blond. I stared in agitation from one to the other and then I panicked. Terrified, I speculated wildly. What do they want with me, and where am I? I became frantic and tried to escape to the top of the bed. As far away as possible from my captors.

The sandy haired man handed me a glass of water, but I was too frightened to drink it. *What if it was drugged?* I thought, in panicked paranoia.

The blond began to speak in a soft, distinct voice. He introduced himself as Aston, pointed to the sandy haired man, stating that his name was Leon. Finally, nodding to my left he said, "Vanda". Each gave me a slight nod, but I still couldn't respond.

Where the hell have they brought me to, and why? How on earth did they know my name was Alex?

They continued to stare as if fascinated by me, and my thoughts once again became chaotic.

I think Aston realised I wasn't getting any calmer, but quite the reverse, as I was now shaking so violently my teeth chattered. He spoke again in a slow, clear voice, in such a strange accent I considered it might be European. Yet his words were clear and concise.

"Alex, you need to calm down and sip some of the water. None of us will harm you. We could never harm you, but quite the reverse. Our intent is to take care of you, and protect you, from now on."

Oh, oh, that was the wrong thing to say. Now, in my head I was thinking, What? I assumed that I had been kidnapped by some foreign gang and about to be abused by them all. Not good at all. I wildly speculated. The news had recently been full of such instances of late.

Vanda then began to speak, "Look at me Alex, and focus on me."

I turned and gazed into those beautiful violet eyes, and became powerless to turn away. Mesmerised, as if set in stone, I slowly began to relax. My breathing becoming more even. Yet unable to comprehend why this was happening.

Wanting to look away, my body not capable of cooperating, I remained transfixed.

Aston spoke again. "We are not on your earth any more Alex. We are on a planet called Syros, in a galaxy far from yours. Do you remember a strange popping noise? Well, that was a portal opening from our planet to yours. It acts as kind of wormhole through space, so we can move with ease from our universe to yours. We have been visiting your planet for millennia."

CAN I ASK A FAVOUR?

If you enjoyed this book, found it useful or otherwise, then I'd really appreciate it if you would post a short review on Amazon. I do read all the reviews personally so that I can continually write what people are wanting.

You can find me on twitter @ScarlettFlame2
Facebook ScarlettFlame2
missscarlettflame.blogspot.co.uk
uk.pinterest.com/redgirl876/
instagram.com/scarlettflame2/
ScarlettFlame.com

Love n stuff
Scarlett
xXx

Printed in April 2023
by Rotomail Italia S.p.A., Vignate (MI) - Italy